A COVEN OF WOMEN

A
COVEN
OF
WOMEN

JEAN BRODY

ATHENEUM

NEW YORK

1987

This novel is a work of fiction. Names, characters, places, and incidents are either the product of the author's imagination or are used fictitiously. Any resemblance to actual events or persons, living or dead, is entirely coincidental.

Library of Congress Cataloging-in-Publication Data

Brody, Jean.
A coven of women.

I. Title.
PS3552.R625C6   1987   813'.54   86-47948
ISBN 0-689-11863-5

Copyright © 1987 by Jean Brody
All rights reserved
Published simultaneously in Canada by Collier Macmillan Canada, Inc.
Composition by Maryland Linotype Composition, Co., Baltimore, Maryland
Manufactured by Fairfield Graphics, Fairfield, Pennsylvania
Designed by Cathryn Aison

FIRST EDITION

For my sons
DAVID AND MATTHEW

Tout aboutit en un livre.

—Stéphane Mallarmé (1842–1898)

VIDA AUSTIN – TEACHER

Born 1890, Robina County, Oklahoma

You have bred discontent in these cold winter people
and caused their young to dream of spring.

CHAPTER ONE

MY AUNT VIDA WAS SIX YEARS OLD WHEN SHE BEGAN COLLECT-ing dead people. In the seventy-four years that followed she gathered up seven in all, not to mention a curious assortment of both wild and domestic animals. There were people here and there who knew something queer was going on but I was the only one who heard the whole truth of it; Aunt Vida's truth, at least, and the truth that I myself imagine.

She propped herself up that day like the withering gladiolas that grew in defiance of the season just outside her bedroom window, brown and dry at the edges but still alive and determined at the center. She lifted a hand swollen with what was killing her and beckoned for me to come close. I put my ear next to her mouth, brushing lips drawn down in a cobweb circle.

"Mary Megan," she whispered, "I want to tell you a secret."

Aunt Vida was actually my great aunt, my Grampa's sister on my father's side. She was the oldest of twelve children, spawned during a time and of a circumstance when a man measured his wealth by the amount of acreage he put under cultivation, how many head of livestock he ran, and the number of sons he could beget before his wife died or went through the change. Great-grandfather Austin sired, to his embarrassment and dismay, four more girls in the six fruitful years after Vida was born, and in spite of my great-grandmother's fervent coital prayers, four more in the middle of the second batch. Not all of them lived, of course; they never did in those days. But still, by local standards, my great-grandfather's seed was sorely afflicted.

In a gallant effort to make the best of a bad situation, he raised the older girls like boys: taught them to plant and to harvest, to ride, shoot, hunt, fish, butcher, chop wood, swear, and divine water. Probably as a result of this extraordinary up-bringing, the two eldest never married, even though according to the portraits in the family Bible they were unusually hand-some young women.

Aunt Vida often said, with a deliciously wicked chuckle, that she and Elizabeth scared the living daylights out of the few men who got up the necessary gumption to come calling. This was due partly to Elizabeth's tongue which, according to Vida, was sharpened every morning before breakfast on the whetstone, and suffered neither the foolish nor the ineptly well-meaning. Vida's shortcoming was her impressive size. Even at eighty, shrunk by time and illness, she stood just under six feet in her silk stockings and weighed close to a hundred and fifty pounds. All bone and sinew, Vida Austin never had so much as a flabby thought.

The collecting began with Vida's grandmother. The old lady was laid out in the parlor in her black Sunday dress, her hands crossed on her bosom. Lily of the Valley cologne mingled sickly sweet with the smell of fleeting flesh, hastened and sea-soned by late July heat.

"I *told* you, your gramma's going to Heaven," her mother answered sharply, weary of so much company and cooking.

"Where's that?" Vida persisted. "Where's Heaven?"

"With our Lord Jesus, that's where."

"But *where*?"

"Where He is. Heaven is wherever He is."

Vida pondered this, then pulled again at her mother's elbow. "How'll she get there, Momma? How do you get to Heaven from Oklahoma?"

"Oh Vida, for landsake! When the preacher says the words, the Angel of the Lord will come for her soul." She wiped her hands on her apron, put one hand on Vida's shoulder, and aimed her toward the door. "You go on along now, you hear? Your momma's busy."

That night Vida puzzled with Elizabeth about the routes to Heaven and why grownups appeared so vague and uncertain as to its exact location. Sleepless and troubled, they slipped into the parlor and carefully hooked Gramma's spectacles over her ears. Why, Gramma couldn't even get across the room without her glasses, let alone to some far-off place she'd never been.

This act satisfied Elizabeth and she slept soundly. Not so Vida. She and the Angel of the Lord grappled for her faith until dawn. Vida, exhausted but victorious, took the pen and ink and paper from her father's desk in the parlor, and she went to him in the kitchen where he sat silently over coffee. Would he write something for her, she wanted to know? Would he write down the words she told him? He smiled the way people do when death is in the next room and he nodded and took the pen.

"It's about Gramma," Vida said. "I want her written down on paper so I won't forget her."

Her father nodded again, dipped the pen in the ink and waited.

Vida said, "Write, 'I loved my gramma. She was always good to me. She never did get mad about little things or walk too fast when we went to town.'" She thought for a moment, then bestowed the highest compliment she could bring to mind. "Put down . . . 'Gramma told good stories.'" And she watched with satisfaction as her father scratched out the words in his fine, graceful script. "Put Vida Anne Austin at the bottom," she said, and added importantly, "age six."

She took the paper from her father, waved it dry, and

went directly to the loft she shared with her sisters. Reverently she placed the words containing Gramma in the wooden box where she kept her smooth stones, snake sheds, and a pleasure-smudged illustrated copy of *The Jungle Book*. She sighed her relief as she closed the lid.

Thereafter whenever she felt her grandmother slipping away, her image and the sound and the feel of her becoming dim, Vida would take the paper from the box and read it over until she was confident that Gramma had settled comfortably into the words and was in no danger of being lured off on some wild-goose chase by the Angel of the Lord.

FOUR YEARS PASSED before a second piece of paper went into the box. New babies were commonplace in the household, but Paul Raymond was special. For one thing he was another much hoped for boy, but that wasn't all of it. He could raise his head up and hold it steady before he was a month old. He walked alone at seven months and spoke in short sentences at one year. Watching him one day, Vida whispered to her mother that Paul Raymond was not brand new.

The winter was a bad one and several of the children took sick. Paul Raymond, the hope and joy of his father, took sickest of all. His breath churned in his throat and he beat himself as if in anger with his tiny balled fists. His mother nursed him through the nights and Vida and Elizabeth divided the days, burning sulfur by his bed, coaxing tonics and herb teas down his narrowed throat. Because he was strong, he was a long time dying.

Vida wrote: "Paul Raymond is to leave for Heaven today. Momma says all babies go directly there because they are without sin. But she still doesn't know where it is or how to get there, so it's the same as with Gramma. I want to say that Paul Raymond was the best baby we ever had. He just slept and ate and played and hardly ever cried. He would lie on the grass in the dooryard and watch the birds and squirrels and they would come close and watch him back and they wouldn't be afraid. If Paul Raymond had grown up to be a man I think he would have done something very grand with his life."

BY THE TIME Vida was eighteen, three more people had been placed with solemn ceremony in the wooden box: her mother, who died of too much work and too little joy; her best friend, Elsie, taken with consumption; and her teacher, Miss Daisy Kretch, who had spent the waning energy of her last years on Vida's education for "better things." All were written down and so spared a doubtful Hereafter.

Soon after the death of Miss Daisy, Vida took a teaching job in a neighboring county where the elders directed her to instruct their children only in what was necessary. Three hours a day was all the time that could be spared from farming, and further, the children were to take no pleasure in what they learned.

It was a poor community; poor in soil and poor in spirit. Crops grew reluctantly. Likewise the seeds of knowledge planted with care by the enthusiastic young teacher died quickly from parental scorn and neglect.

In the second year, Vida was courted by a six-foot-five-inch widower who admired her glorious bosom enough to overlook both her native and acquired intelligence. But then one afternoon he called for her at the schoolhouse and found her sweating and swearing as she bolted a new stove through a metal sheet to the wood floor. There was a newly sawed hole for the pipe, and a quarter cord of new-cut walnut was stacked in the corner of the room. A few months later the widower married the local milliner, a frail and delicate lady with less offensive talents.

As time passed Vida turned more and more for company to the people in the wooden box. They were brought out every evening and they gathered around the kitchen table in the small cabin next to the schoolhouse where they talked about the old days and pretended they were better than they were. Paul Raymond played quietly on a quilt spread before the fire; Miss Daisy Kretch read poetry; Gramma rocked and made fine stitches in linens for Vida's hope chest; Momma hummed over a bucket of apples or peaches for the next day's pie; and Vida and Elsie whispered and giggled secrets worn thin with telling.

Vida was unfulfilled, but she was not unhappy.

One spring day in Vida's third year at the school the Hawkins boy showed up with an ailing yellow dog and asked if he could leave him there. This was a community where everything that ate, worked. Ten years of devoted service did not guarantee an old yellow dog a place by the fire. Vida took him in. Soon after, a gunny sack mewed and squirmed on the front porch, and not long after that, a young raccoon with a trap-mangled leg was found tied to the railing. In due time, they all found their way into the wooden box.

VIDA WAS ASKED to leave after her seventh year. Word went around that there was something peculiar about the schoolteacher. Voices could be heard coming from the cabin if one passed by on the road at night, and one of the elders swore he heard an infant cry. Most of all they feared for the souls of their children who, in direct disobedience of their orders, were actually receiving enjoyment from the schooling.

"What have I done wrong, Miss Daisy?"

"You are educating them, Vida," Miss Kretch answered matter-of-factly.

"But I'm a teacher; that's what I'm supposed to do."

"They told you, Vida, they told you exactly what they wanted: children who could do their sums to a hundred and order out of the Sears catalogue. Instead, you've opened their eyes to better things. You have bred discontent in these cold winter people and caused their young to dream of spring."

Vida gazed down at her feet. "I have failed to honor my agreement."

"Failed! Agreement! Honor!" Miss Daisy was outraged. "Words with no spleen! You have no need of them, Vida Austin. Yours is a high destiny. You have changed the course of history in Cheney, Oklahoma."

VIDA PACKED her belongings and because she had no place else to go, went home to the farm where she found her sister Elizabeth growing old and twisted with the same endless labor that had killed their mother.

"Talk to her, Vida," her mother said. "See if you can't convince her to go to Kansas City and take nurse's training, or go in for teaching like you, or marry that nice fellow who comes around—the one from the hardware store. Anything to get the poor soul away from here."

Vida frowned. "I can't do that, Momma. Who'd take care of Papa and the children? If Elizabeth left then we'd have to stay on." She sighed, partly in annoyance with herself. "I guess that's selfishness on my part, but she wouldn't leave anyway. I know it. She says the Lord has shone His light on her duty. She won't leave this place as long as Papa's alive."

Her mother's eyes widened and her hand fluttered to her breast. "Oh Vida," she cried in a trembling voice, "you've got to promise me! When that happens, when that man dies you have got to let him go to Heaven!"

VIDA'S PEOPLE did not like it at the farm. They complained about being shut up in the box so much of the time, and that the loft was drafty and unpleasant when they were let out. They missed the evenings around the table with the fire roaring in the iron stove and the yellow dog lying at their feet. Vida finally found work as a governess in the home of a gentleman farmer, Malcolm MacGuire, just a few miles north of Claremore. With the position came a small comfortable cottage, away from the main house, a circumstance of which her family heartily approved. The MacGuire children, Virginia and Amy, two spoiled-rotten girls who had watched nurses and governesses come and go for most of their pampered lives, were agile and adept at resisting learning in any form.

"They don't know half the words in the primer," Vida complained to Miss Daisy. "And they know their tables only through the fives!"

"They're just ornery, that's all. You have to get their attention," Miss Daisy advised. "Read to them. Read them something romantic."

So Vida and the girls read *Jane Eyre* together and by the time Bertha Rochester had perished in the fire, Virginia, the quick one, was doing long division and cheerfully diagramming compound sentences, her sister hard on her heels. Malcolm MacGuire was grateful, which he expressed in the form of a raise in pay and a leather-bound set of the complete works of the Brontës. Mrs. MacGuire spoke of her gratitude from her invalid's bed where she spent most of every day, doing fine embroidery and having the neighbor ladies in for tea.

Vida remained in the MacGuires' service for six years. It was whispered about that the situation was to be expected. A man in the prime of life. A handsome, healthy woman. And poor Mrs. MacGuire sick and all . . .

Then one day in late spring, after a lunch shared with Vida and the girls, Malcolm complained of a tightness in his chest, took to his bed, and died before suppertime. Vida wrote long into the night; it took twenty pages to contain him.

"This is best," she wrote. "Malcolm could not have tolerated our deceit for much longer. He would have left her, or killed her; neither solution acceptable to a well-bred gentleman like himself."

She held her pen in midair, tapped it lightly against her chin, and stared into the fire. "Vida Austin," she said, "you are ten kinds of a fool! You've been reading so much of the Sisters Brontë you've got sap coursing through your brains." She put her pen to paper and wrote swiftly and surely. "He would have done neither of those things; he would not have killed her because he was not a violent man; he would not have left her because she's the one with the money." She narrowed her eyes in hard thought. "*This* is what he would have done; this is what would have come to pass: One night when too many brandies had raised his self-pity up to the guilty level, he would have slunk to her bedside and confessed all. Then the poor woman, being tossed back and forth on the horns of pride and convenience, would have been forced to fire me as hussy, having been totally satisfied with my work as hired heart.

"Tomorrow, I will give my notice to Mrs. MacGuire and begin to look for a new place. The girls no longer need me—I congratulate myself on a job well done. They will make their mark, those two, especially Virginia who has an upright mind and the gift of healing in her hands.

"I'm taking Malcolm with me. Momma and Gramma say it's unseemly. They fear for my virtue which they confuse with innocence long gone. Miss Daisy is pleased because he is 'a reader,' and Elsie because he's a noisy man who knows how to laugh and sing and have a good time.

"I'm taking him because I love him. Good a reason as any."

VIDA SENT OFF letters and filled out applications. Then on the first day of August, 1921, she and her family left the broad

Oklahoma plains in a 1915 Model T touring car that Vida learned to drive and maintain along the way. Forty-five days later they chugged into Cadyville, a long rich valley in northern California, born of the logs of great redwoods and nourished with apple orchards and sheep.

She was thirty-one years old when she came to the valley, and ten blissful years went by before she had to leave it. The town council built a larger school for the new teacher and they willingly provided the books she requested. In Cadyville the business of children was to be children, for there was money enough to hire the shearing, picking, and felling.

During the first year, Vida instituted conferences in which she met individually with the parents to discuss the progress or lack of it of her charges. It was during the course of these conferences that Vida came to know Emily Gladkov, née Emily Cady, who owned half the county including the newspaper, of which she was the editor. Vida and Emily found that they delighted in each other's company, and they commenced to go down to Stanford for lectures and seminars, to the city for shopping, and to meet every Tuesday evening for a late supper and spirited discussion about Books and Ideas.

In spite of her numerous obligations and hectic schedule, Emily never missed a parent-teacher conference with Vida, during which time she could be counted on to commit the sin of pride regarding her son, Gregory, and the sin of anger regarding her daughter, Catherine.

"Emily, the girl is *not* dull! I'll not let you say that about her. All of her work is above average."

"But only just, Vida. Only just. I can't understand it. It is beyond my comprehension! She's always under Molly's feet in the kitchen wanting to know how to cook this or that or the other. And, would you believe, she has taught herself to do"— she paused, then spit out the word as if it had soiled her tongue —"*nee-dle-work*."

Vida laughed and shook her head. "Well now, Em, I've not heard tell that cooking and sewing are misdemeanors."

"But she doesn't have to *like* it so much! She has no ambition, Vida, not a modicum; no interest in matters of the mind. Why, she doesn't even want to go to college. Emily Cady's daughter does not want to go to college!"

Vida restrained another laugh and spoke in a serious tone. "Why don't you just leave that to me? Let's see, Catherine is eight now, almost nine? I think I have time to bring her around."

Emily pulled a handkerchief from her sleeve and pressed it to her cheek. Vida steadied herself for the Sarah Bernhardt sketch that was sure to follow. "I can see it now," said Emily. "Catherine will marry some unwashed lumberjack and spawn a houseful of dirty, snotty-nosed children, and *never* have time to open a book." She clutched her chest and slumped against Vida's desk. "My God! My poor *grand*children—my flesh, my blood—destitute and ignorant. Oh Vida! I could just weep!"

Vida placed her hands on Emily's shoulders and looked directly into her eyes. "Why don't you just love her, Emily. Lord knows she's easy to love. Let's divide up the labor here. You do the mothering and I'll do the teaching. I promise you, I give you my solemn word, your daughter will go to college." She stepped back and snapped her fingers with a sudden thought. "I'll speak to Miss Daisy about Catherine. Miss Daisy always has such good ideas."

And thus, Vida began to be careless with her family, and as time passed allowed them the run of the town. Malcolm spent his days in the small public library over the drugstore, then began to make frequent trips to San Francisco where he became an ardent patron of the opera, to be gone for weeks at a time. Vida's grandmother nailed a hand-lettered sign—Dressmaking & Alterations—to the front gate, and her mother commenced to go to the Presbyterian church on Sundays and Wednesday evenings. They all took their rightful places as citizens of the community. The community, in time, grew uneasy.

When Emily traveled back to New Orleans for her college reunion, her husband, Peter, filled in for her at Tuesday

Night Supper, and Books and Ideas. Peter, a handsome American-born Russian who came originally from Mendocino on the coast, was trying—he confided to Vida—had tried for years, at the urging of his valley-born wife, to raise sheep. But his eyes, reared in fog and salted wind, were blinded by the bright inland sun. His hands, so quick to untangle and mend nets, were clumsy with matted wool.

Even after Emily returned, Peter continued to be a frequent visitor in the cottage behind the schoolyard, especially during Malcolm MacGuire's long absences throughout the opera season.

WHEN VIDA LEFT Cadyville, Peter Gladkov was packed with the others in the wooden box, and with him his stories of the time before the great sea harvest when the waters off the California coast were a living blanket of fish, seal, and otter, and when sheep were kept only by cowards and by women.

They moved up and down the Pacific Coast, settling in one town after another as Vida's services were no longer required, until finally Elsie's consumption forced them into the desert. The moving was hardest on Vida's mother, who needed a town and a church, and a place to plant and harvest.

"Why do we always have to *leave*? I no more than get my potatoes in the ground than you whisk us off to someplace else."

Vida would reach across the table and cover her mother's hand with her own. "Because we're different, Momma. Don't worry, I'll find us a place."

And it seemed that she had found one, desolate though it was and with scant hope for potatoes. For seven years she taught at the Indian school on the Apache reservation near Phoenix. The chief welcomed not only the handsome, smiling teacher but also her companions, and the Indian school enjoyed a success that had not been visited on it in the past. Vida's version of American history was so close to the truth as to be interesting, and did not, like so many others, begin with the landing of the *Mayflower*. The student population outgrew the twelve-by-twelve shack to which it had been assigned and included, in addition to the children who were required to attend, several grown men and women.

A new building was constructed, not without endless correspondence between Vida and the Bureau of Indian Affairs. And a second teacher was hired. They were lucky to get him, Vida told the chief after his meeting with Simon Cole, a newly widowered professor of English from the University of California in Santa Barbara. When the chief questioned why a man so weighted with honors would come to teach in a poor Indian school, Vida explained that Professor Cole's heart was heavier than his credentials and needed a place where it could be lightened of its burden; that his mind, though it soared like a falcon, was fragile from many blows and wanted a safe eyrie in which to rest.

Simon Cole brought with him to the desert his three children, Regina, Claudia, and the youngest, Dorian—his favorite—who was the sweet golden image of her dead mother. *Jane Eyre* was not obliged to whet the intellectual appetites of the Cole girls. Rather, Vida found herself happily scrambling to keep ahead of them, especially the eldest, Regina, who drank up Vida's lessons like a saguaro in a spring rain.

Simon was ten years younger, a full three inches shorter, and twenty pounds lighter than Vida but was a giant in his passions—Vida's equal in that way. After a few months had gone by they began to meet together in the evenings and engage in lively discussions about Books and Ideas. So much did Vida treasure Simon's company that on these occasions she kept her family shut up in the wooden box. At length they began to grumble that they were ignored and abandoned, but Vida was as one blessed, and the months changed as if by magic into years.

One evening after Books and Ideas, Simon and Vida took

a stroll out under the stars and Simon gravely asked Vida to give him the honor of her hand in marriage.

"Our bodies are surely married by now," she told him. "And we have a union of the spirit."

But Simon wanted a more formal arrangement, to take her to Santa Barbara as his bride, to resume his duties at the university, to live again in the real world. He had talked it over with the girls, and they would like nothing better than to welcome Vida into their family circle.

"I'll have to think about it, Simon. I'm fifty-two years old, a little long in the tooth to take up wifing and mothering. I'll have to give it some thought."

The more she thought about it, the more she liked the idea. Why shouldn't she have a husband like other women, especially one so cherished. Why shouldn't she have a home where children came in from school and told about their day? To have at last the long-promised "place" for her mother's garden.

She told Simon that she would marry him and go with him back to Santa Barbara. He was to come that evening to her lodge for a celebration dinner.

Should he bring the girls? the happiest of all men wanted to know.

No, not this time. Vida wanted him to meet *her* family.

VIDA AND SIMON left the reservation, but not together. Vida resumed her search for a place: mining towns, lumber towns, farming towns, towns with no real reason to be, she tried them all. Animals dead of wheels, predation, and time went into the box until at last her gramma complained generally about overcrowding and in particular about the goat—and made Vida promise to collect no more.

The year she broke her hip in a fall off of a spooked horse, she came to stay with my grandfather on his ranch near Tucson. She was in her early seventies then, slowed down some but not stopped by any means. Her hearing was not what it had been, but her eyes and her mind were still sharp enough for the small print of her Shakespeare.

Every spring, the day after school let out, I'd be put on the Greyhound in Dallas to be picked up by Grampa at the station in Tucson. And so would begin an endless, shoeless, bookless summer; or so it was until Aunt Vida broke her hip. It was clear to her on first meeting that the Dallas public school system had failed to get through to me, and almost on the spot *Jane Eyre* was once again pressed into service.

There was the Greek Summer (Homer mostly), the Dickens Summer—shared with Fielding and a little Hardy— and the Russian Summer (Peter's idea, likely). The French Summer caused bad feelings between my mother and Aunt Vida, my mother contending that *Madame Bovary* was not proper reading for a girl of my sheltered sensibilities. The Poetry Summer was the best; I wept exuberant, satisfying tears over the Brownings and their deathless devotion to each other. I was fourteen, sprouting bosoms and hormones, and counting the ways I loved Billy Bob Cooper.

The Thoreau Summer was the last. Lessons were conducted at Aunt Vida's bedside and consisted mostly of my reading aloud while she dozed, rousing herself the moment my mind wandered out of *Walden* with, "And how would you say that in your own words, Mary Megan?"

Toward the end of August, Grampa began to mope about the place saying he just didn't like the looks of it—no sir!—she was failing all right. She told him she wouldn't have it but he got the doctor out from town anyway. The doctor inched his stethoscope over Aunt Vida's still ample chest, then patted her hand and told her she was coming along nicely. Aunt Vida laughed and called him a quack, then after he was gone, leaving behind a supply of pills and capsules, motioned for me to come close.

"Mary Megan," she whispered, "I want to tell you a secret . . ."

I took the wooden box as she instructed from the top shelf of the closet and carried it to the bed. She opened the top slowly and smiled a greeting at the vapors that floated gently out. I didn't breathe, didn't stir, just sat there struck dumb and watched the mist take on shapes and settle on the quilt around her. I took the stack of papers from the box in shaking hands and while Aunt Vida slept, read until the darkness crept in through the east window.

Aunt Vida's voice came from the pillow, muffled and faint. "You must set them free, Mary Megan. I'm so tired—so very tired. I suppose I've used up my life."

I burst out in tears. "Oh no, Aunt Vida!"

She looked at me from the corner of her eye. "Come on now, girl, none of that. My death is important to me. I'll not make it less than it is by pretending it isn't going to happen. What is it that Mister Thoreau says about facing a fact?" She waited patiently but my mind could not locate my tongue. She sighed. " 'If you stand face to face with a fact, you will see the sun glimmer on both its surfaces, and its sweet edge dividing you through the heart and marrow . . .' " She paused, waiting for her lagging student to catch up.

" '. . . and so,' " I quoted, sniffing loudly, " 'you will happily conclude your mortal career.' Oh Aunt Vida . . .!"

"The last line, Mary Megan. *Let us hear* the last line."

" 'Let us hear,' " I repeated after her, " 'let us hear *the rattle*—'?"

"If—?"

"Oh. 'If we are really dying—' " That was the problem, I had blocked on "dying." I took a deep breath and started over. " 'If we are really dying, let us hear the rattle in our throats and feel cold in the extremities; if we are alive, let us go about our business.' "

Aunt Vida smiled—that singular blessing—and I did too, through my tears, because I had not failed her. She reached out and touched my face. "Now, you do as I say, hear?"

She gave directions in the crisp, schoolteacher voice she used for nonnegotiables. I was to burn the pages in the fireplace, one by one, and I was to take special care with Malcolm and with Peter. Certain of our relations, my mother in particular, were unsympathetic to lapses of the flesh.

I kept my back to her while I did it; I could not bear to see her face. My hand trembled as I put the match to Peter Gladkov and his tales of the California sea. And did I imagine it, or did Miss Daisy really burn brighter than the rest?

WE BURIED Aunt Vida in early September, just before I returned to the university. There was a handwritten will in which the wooden box and Aunt Vida's books came to me. She had little else to leave. Grampa sold the ranch that fall to a real estate development company and moved to a fancy place for senior citizens in San Diego. I took it very personally, his selling the ranch. As I saw it, he sold the best part of my childhood, and my girlhood, and my coming of age. The enchanted Browning Summer was bulldozed, razed, flattened, and covered over with rows of three-bedroom, two-bath reality.

A year later I got my degree in journalism, and in spite of my mother's objections to the place (rapists, murderers, homosexuals, crazy people, fortune hunters, liars, cheats, foreigners, movie stars, Democrats, and—I don't know how she came up with this one—unlicensed mad dogs), I came out to California to find my destiny.

I thought a lot about Aunt Vida in the beginning—carried her memory with me as an amulet that protected me and reminded me to be brave, especially when I was running out of jobs to apply for and was wondering how it felt to be *really* hungry. I had twenty dollars and fifty-three cents left in my purse when United Press saw fit to hire me. I knew Aunt Vida would be proud—I hadn't written home for money.

Then as time went by, the image and the sound and the feel of her began to grow dim from lack of use. I found I had to squeeze my eyes shut and be very patient and sit quietly before I could conjure her up: the green eyeshade riding low on her brow; her thumb and forefinger framing her chin; her eyes coaxing, waiting; her large, strong body tensed with the hope that the miracle of understanding was taking place.

And then about a year ago, soon after my thirty-first birthday, I squeezed my eyes shut again and again, but she wouldn't come. Vida was gone and I needed the memory of her as I never had before. I needed the example of her strength and independence and passion for life to get me through an impasse, a time of desolate confusion and hard choices.

Five years ago, when Ricky and I moved in together, we agreed—sensibly, we said—that marriage was an unnecessary legality because neither of us wanted children. Ricky has a son by his first wife, and I had determined early on to devote my life to my career. But one morning, after that wretched birthday, on my way to work I dropped off a baby gift at a friend's. She was nursing the baby when I got there and asked me to wait a bit so we could have coffee and a chat. I sat across from them watching what I told myself archly was a primitive display, and then all of a great sudden, I felt my own breasts filling. I held the baby, I burped the baby, I cooed at the baby, I took the baby's toes to market. I was late to work, which didn't matter much, because I didn't take my head with me anyway.

That night I told Ricky I had changed my mind about children. He said if that was really so, I had the wrong man. He reminded me of our agreement; he reminded me that we had planned a trip to Greece; he reminded me that a child consumes about two decades of its mother's time.

That's when I started thinking about Aunt Vida, about how her work had sustained and nourished her life—a life that required neither husband nor child to give it meaning. I needed to know more about that life.

So, on a typical southern California June morning—bleak and overcast—I prepared to do battle with the Angel of the Lord. I got the wooden box down from the top shelf of my closet and began to fill it with the secrets Vida had told me the summer before she died, and although the old woman struggled like a caught bird against rescue, I finally wrestled what I knew of her into it.

Something curious and magical happened in the process. As I became more and more entangled in the threads of Vida's story, I thought less and less about the baby. I wanted to know more about the lives Vida had touched, some with abiding grace, some to wound beyond healing. I was obsessed with the words left unsaid, the deeds unaccounted for, the lapses, the inconsistencies. Ah! Vida had not told me all her secrets. As heiress to the wooden box I began to divine them—to write between the lines. How did Peter die? Why did Vida leave Cadyville? Did Elizabeth stay on the farm and live her whole life as a moral duty? Did Catherine marry a lumberjack and have a houseful of children, or did she go to college as Vida promised Emily she would? Did Virginia make her mark? Did Simon take the children with him when he left the reservation? And what of those children? Homer says the gods weave misfortunes so the generations to come will have something to sing about.

I fell under a spell, rising before the sun every morning to see what songs the day would bring. And that's how this all came about; that's how I started collecting on my own.

EMILY CADY GLADKOV—EDITOR

Born 1885, Cadyville, California

Vida and Emily found that they delighted in each other's company, and they commenced to go down to Stanford for lectures and seminars, to the city for shopping, and to meet every Tuesday evening for a late supper and spirited discussion about Books and Ideas.

CHAPTER TWO

Emily Cady Gladkov watched with dry-eyed satisfaction as the redwood casket bearing the shattered body of her husband was lowered into the ground. The reverend held out the shovel to her for the ritual handful of dust. She took it from him briskly and tossed its entire contents into the grave. Slowly, deliberately, she thrust it into the loose mound near her feet and flung another and then another and yet another shovelful of dirt into the last resting place of the man who had shared her bed for twenty-five years.

She had wished him dead, and it had come to pass. She had willed it with an awesome energy which had found expression in the runaway logging truck that struck him down in the darkness as he crossed the highway in front of the schoolyard.

"Mother . . .?" Gently, Gregory took the shovel from her and returned it to the open-mouthed minister. "Let's go home now," he said quietly, coaxing her as one would a difficult child prone to outbursts of temper. "People will be coming by. It's time to go now."

Catherine, the daughter, stood to the son's right, one hand extended toward her mother, the other pressing a damp white handkerchief against her cheek. "It's time to go now," she echoed.

"You knew," Emily said to them, ignoring her daughter's outstretched hand. "They knew," she added harshly, and lifted her arm toward the graveside assemblage. And with both arms wide spread she hissed under her breath, "The whole valley knew." The blue ice of her eyes fell and froze on one of the mourners—the schoolteacher, a tall veiled figure standing apart from the rest.

Firmly, Gregory put one arm around his mother's shoulders and guided her away from the graveside. Catherine moved ahead of them, her footfalls rapid crunches on the gravel, to the row of cars at the top of the rise. She opened the door on the passenger side and stepped back, servile, her white-knuckled hands clutching her purse to her breast.

When they had crossed the road, Emily shook off her son's arm. "You've been laughing at me," she announced in a flat, toneless voice. "Laughing, that's what!"

"No, Mother," her son said, shaking his head. And with a hint of wryness, he added, "You have never given us cause to laugh at you."

In the silence that followed, Emily considered this remark, and the source of it. Her son stood before her in his father's outdoor skin, molded firmly over his father's sharp facial planes, his hard muscles, his long, loosely joined bones. The dark eyes that met hers squarely, those too were Peter Gladkov's. Gregory was all sperm. The egg had paused in its obligatory passage through Emily's fallopian tube to accept the fast-swimming winner of the race for immortality, and then— so it seemed—had contributed nothing further.

"Pity, then," she amended, spitting it out like a bitter seed. "You pitied me while he consorted with that Amazon whore!"

The daughter began to cry. Tears slipped from her light eyes onto her transparent cheeks and fell to her fragile collarbones. In Catherine, at least, the egg had asserted itself. "Please Mother," she pleaded. "Daddy is dead. We have just buried my daddy. Please, I want to go home."

Emily made no sign she had heard as she walked around the car to the driver's side. She motioned with her head toward the crowd moving in slow cadence away from the grave and up the hill.

"Get a ride with someone," she said. "I have work to do at the paper." A fleeting smile parted her lips as she slid purposefully behind the wheel. "I have an obituary to write . . ."

THE MAIN STREET of Cadyville was quiet, and except for a dusty pickup truck parked in front of Clara's Bar and Grill, it was deserted. The town, as it always did, had closed down to observe the passing of one of its own.

Emily pulled the long, sleek LaSalle into the place reserved for it in the alley behind the newspaper office. She took the key from the ignition, sighed heavily, and leaned her head on the back of the seat. The editor, she thought, the last to get the news. But Oh dear God, the worst thing, the worst thing of all! To live with a man all those years, to lie down with him in wonder, in passion, in friendship, in habit, in boredom, in anger—each in its own time—then at the end of it to have no tears for the loss of him.

She shook her head, stirred herself. "Their doing," she said aloud. "Peter's and Vida's. Not mine."

Inside, the office was cool and dark. Emily adjusted the blinds to let the midmorning September sun stream across her desk, then she lit the gas jet under coffee left from the day before. She pulled the dark blue cloche from her head and hung it, with her navy silk jacket, on the clothes tree in the corner.

She was a striking woman; everyone, even those who were not beholden to her, said so. Too small and finely formed to be called handsome, but with features too well defined for prettiness. Her eyes were a bright clear blue, round and alert in her smooth face which seemed whiter for the dark bobbed hair combed neatly around it. Vigor, discipline, and probably her metabolic constitution had kept her body slim and bend-some; even her breasts had resisted the downward pull of time and gravity. Vanity and small laughter had preserved her face as a protective mask slipped into place each morning. Peter, not long before the accident, had told her that she was beautiful when she slept. Like many of his compliments—at least he said they were compliments—she had taken this as personal criticism.

Steam rose from the pot and she poured the coffee, black and thick, into a white mug, then she slumped heavily into her swivel chair. The Cadyville *Clarion* had begun its life as a hobby, her late father's monthly newsletter to the community, but when Emily returned from her mother's native New Orleans after four years at Sophie Newcomb College, armed with a degree in English and a gnawing need to reshape the world, the paper evolved into a weekly, and as a result of her energy, her talent, and her father's awe of her, over the years had earned a reputation for excellence. William Allen White was one of Emily's admirers. And over her desk hung a framed letter from vice-presidential candidate Franklin Roose-velt, commending her on her eloquent essay in support of the League of Nations.

Emily was twenty-nine years old when her parents died in a boating accident. As their only child she inherited the *Clarion*, along with five thousand acres of redwood forest and a near equal amount of prime bottom land—apple land, sheep land—that stretched from Cadyville to the sea. The young wife/mother/part-time editor was instantly transformed into matriarch and she wore the cloak of sovereignty like a queen born to the royal robes. No one would have dared to sow wild oats in her fields, poach her forest, hang horns on her door.

THE *Clarion* had been put to bed by her two-man staff the night before. She would rouse it to add one item of local interest.

She rolled a sheet of blank paper into the Remington, centered it, then backspaced. The words "In Memory" were clicked off, then silence except for the sound of the chair swiveling thoughtfully back and forth. Memory. Pages in the mind full of vagaries, murky imagery, illusions, half-remembered conversations, half-forgotten events, all edited and rewritten by the passage of time.

Emily's obituaries were cherished by the families of Cadyville's deceased. She allowed kindly shadows to obscure meanness or failure, letting the light fall full on whatever deeds or qualities were praiseworthy. Once Clara had told her lunchtime customers at the Bar and Grill, "Why, it's almost worth the dyin' to have ol' Emily write you up."

Cadyville's skeletons rattled and clanked in her mind's closet from time to time, but the town along with its inhabitants she saw as an extension of herself and therefore immune to negative scrutiny. Further, Aaron Potter's occasional shoplifting at Ramsey's Hardware was a minor transgression when put alongside the hideous theft that was going on in Hitler's Germany; the town's one indigent panhandler was insignificant when compared with the four and a half million Americans out of work—the direct result, Emily had written, of Herbert Hoover's Smoot-Hawley Tariff bill which had caused the decline of world trade and led to international depression. The valley's shortcomings and problems paled when likened to those evils that existed in the outside world. The four horsemen rode savagely and relentlessly over the earth—yes—but they were not allowed to linger in Cadyville.

She took a deep breath and ran her fingertips over the keys. She rotated the roller, reversed the ribbon, and peered inside to see that the type slugs were clean. With her well-manicured finger on the lever, she moved the carriage into position. Then she stroked the machine as a hunter caresses the barrel of his gun in the early dawn.

And she fired:

Peter Serge Gladkov was born in Mendocino in 1880. He was the son of Natasha Gladkov who came to California just two months before his birth. Madame Gladkov won the respect of the entire community when it became known that she and Peter's father, members of the People's Freedom Party in Russia, had taken part in the bombing of the imperial dining room in the Winter Palace. She won its sympathy when it was learned that her husband had been imprisoned and later executed following the Winter Palace incident, and that she, the tragic, expectant mother, had narrowly escaped a like fate when fellow party members spirited her out of St. Petersburg and into the United States.

This is the story that Cadyville has accepted for many years. But an investigation into the matter reveals the following facts: Natasha Gladkov, an uneducated (but nonetheless imaginative) girl with no political leanings one way or the other, was the daughter of an Alaskan fur trader. She was sent by her father to his sister in Mendocino when Natasha's illicit pregnancy became known to him . . .

Emily hunched over her typewriter, her thin hands clutching at her knees, and she read aloud the words she had written. They fell heavily onto the silence; hollow, impotent rhetoric with no power to punish the dead.

"Why?" she moaned. "Oh God, Peter, *why?*" Her arms folded themselves on the cool black metal and she rested her chin upon them. "We had a good life together," she murmured. "We were happy . . ."

She dozed, she must have dozed she decided, because the slanted stream of sunlight was gone when she raised her head, the air inside the office damp and grey. She yawned, stretched, and rolled her head slowly on the stiff pillar of her neck, and turned back to her work. There, splashed randomly across the newsprint, was a long belly laugh. Line after line of "Ha" and "Ho" and "Hee," punctuated with dashes and slashes and question marks, terminated finally in the upper-case words: HAPPY?? HAPPY!! HOW LONG, EMILY, HOW

LONG SINCE YOU AND PETER HAVE BEEN
HAPPY???#*??!

A black-dotted rush of adrenaline pushed the chair away
from the desk, lifted her body up, and sent it stumbling toward the door. Her fingers fumbled for the bolt, then she
stopped and turned. "Who's here?" she whispered. "Who is
it?" Her shoulders rose and fell with her short, rapid breaths.
A fly, buzzing its own obituary, was the only living sound in
the room.

On tiptoe, Emily crept back to her desk, pulled up the
chair, and eased into it. "Who are you?" her fingers demanded
of the Remington.

The answer came back quickly. "I am your faithful
servant, Emily. I live here in this black machine and I do your
bidding. I strike this platen with your passion, even unto your
platitudes."

"Oh now, just a minute!" Emily snapped. "This is insanity. I'm not going to do this."

"It is a perfectly acceptable form. Dickens used it. And
Dante. And that man in New York with his cockroach."

Emily covered her eyes and peered through the spaces
between her fingers. "This is insanity," she repeated.

"I have told you it is perfectly acceptable," the machine
insisted. "The typewriter, like its predecessor the pen, is a useful tool for analyzing one's self and one's fellows. Twenty-six
lettered keys to unlock the doors to the dark closets of the heart.
If you were a novelist you would simply bring in your cast of
characters, set them on a course whereby they would define the
eternal triangle, and you would, in the process, discover the
cause and implications of your tragic betrayal.

"Here, let me just show you how it works: We find Peter
and Emily in the dulling, deadly act of living happily ever
after. Peter, the bronzed god, the disenfranchised fisherman,
telling his tales, repairing them, retying the knots, battening
down the arguments, mourning the sea. He hates sheep. He

despises forests unless they've been cut up and made boats of; his beloved children have gone away to school; and his wife is prone to headaches after nine o'clock in the evening, as a result of which he approaches her for sexual solace rarely and reticently.

"Lord knows that suits Emily fine. She's weary of it, the same old ritual beginning with a hardness to the small of the back, a hand to the left breast, cool pursed lips to the right one (God! Has that man lost his tongue!), and ending soon afterward with a hasty jabbing, an involuntary gasp, and a muttered apology.

"Emily—our heiress, graduate of Sophie Newcomb, queen mother of Cadyville—runs everything, the town, the children, the newspaper, the redwood empire—and Peter, to whom she has assigned the ignoble (in his eyes) task of running the sheep. In summary, they have taken small, polite bites of their days and nights together, and thus have nibbled away at the years.

"Enter Vida, one-hundred-and-sixty-pound fairy princess. She listens to Peter's tale, she mends his tattered dreams. She weaves a magic cloth of them, and in the woof she puts the sunsets and the evening star and the soft night air and the spring rain. In the warp goes her thick unpinned hair, her smooth grasping thighs, her Viking breasts. She sets this cloth like a sail on the air where it floats, trembles, hovers, then settles sweetly above them, and beneath these woven dreams, together they create the mighty ocean."

Abruptly, Emily turned her palms upward and inspected them closely. Wondrous instruments for weaving. See how neatly each finger bends at its three perfectly spaced joints. How the thumb, that unique treasure, sweeps effortlessly from one side of the hand to the other. And the plump, scrolled tips, sensory inspection team, tender translators of silent messages.

Twenty-eight years before when a full summer moon had guided both the tide and their naked bodies to a rendezvous on the sand at the ocean's edge, she had written with these very fingertips *I love you* in virginal delicacy across his chest, and then traced it again, brazenly, joyfully, from navel to groin. And the waves had crashed upon the rocks, the white caps bowing and retreating in tribute to this most perfect of all loves.

Emily closed her eyes. "Is it the same ocean?" she whispered.

"Oh yes, the same. The very same. And the same full moon, the same tide. It is, my dear, the same old tale."

The sound of knocking came from the rear of the office, polite at first with long pauses in between, then a loud, impatient rapping, which Emily, sitting quiet and cold as a stone, continued to ignore. A face, shading itself with both hands cupped around it, appeared through the black-and-gold lettering on the front window. With slow, reluctant steps, Emily went to the door. She slid the bolt then stepped back, her head cocked to one side, her arms folded under her breasts.

Vida Austin filled the open doorway. Black became her; it softened her voluptous dimensions, enhanced the coiled rope of red-gold hair. She moved forward, placed her hands on Emily's shoulders, and bent to kiss her cheek.

"Gregory said you were working."

"Yes, I'm working."

"Really Emily! Today?" She walked purposefully to the clothes tree. Collecting the jacket and hat, she said, "You have to come home now. Catherine is bereaved. She needs you, she needs her momma."

"She needs her momma," said Emily, mimicking Vida's soft drawl. "And where's the momma to comfort me? Humph! We all learn to do without a momma."

"That's true, Emily," Vida snapped, "but I think you might give the child notice before you resign the position."

Emily took the hat and jacket and returned them to the clothes tree. "How good of you, Vida," she said. "A little friend-of-the-family errand. How very kind and thoughtful. Would the friend of the family like some coffee?" Vida blinked, then nodded. "It's yesterday's," Emily went on, and without asking added two heaping teaspoons of sugar to the cup. "Have a chair, won't you?" She stirred the coffee before handing over the mug.

Vida accepted the cup and the chair with murmured thanks, then took a sip of the coffee. "Just right," she smiled.

Emily shrugged and sat down at her desk.

Vida cleared her throat. "So?"

"So?"

"Well." She indicated the typewriter with a nod of her head. "What are you up to that won't keep for a few days?"

"So Gregory didn't tell you? I'm writing Peter's obit, not having much luck with it." She leaned forward and looked directly into Vida's eyes. "It appears that I didn't know him as well as I thought I did."

Vida sighed, settled back in the chair, and took a thin silver case from her bag. She removed a cigarette, tapped it on the case, and lit it. The smoke hung on the silence between them. "All right, Em," she said finally. "Let's not go all the way around the barn to get to this."

Emily smoothed the folds in her skirt and picked at a loose thread in the hem. "I don't know quite where one begins in these things," she said quietly. Then in a voice weighted with sarcasm, she added, "But in view of our old and valued friendship it would seem to me that you owe me some sort of explanation." To her surprise, her voice cracked and fell on the last words, and with it her stiff-backed reserve. "How could you do that to me, Vida?" she cried out. "I've been your friend all these years. I got you the new school, the library you asked for, the scholarships, the gym! Whatever you wanted, I saw to it that you got it."

Vida nodded agreeably. "I know that, Em, and I'm very grateful to you."

Emily went on as if she hadn't heard. "I protect you. I

defend you when people say you're—well, *peculiar*. And how
do you repay my friendship? You take my husband as your
lover!" Suddenly the skin around her jaw sagged and her face
was like a negative plunged into developing solution, as slowly,
irreversibly, thin lines appeared on her cheeks, around her
eyes, above her mouth.

Vida leaned forward and covered Emily's clenched hands
with her own. "I'm sorry—Oh Lord!—I'm so sorry, Emily. I
didn't think you cared. You hadn't paid that man any mind
for so long I didn't think you cared anymore."

Emily's eyes widened as she pulled out of Vida's grasp.
"Didn't care?" she whimpered. "Didn't *care?*"

"Well. You've tended to everything else in sight but him.
Been so busy trying to get Herbert Hoover out of office you
didn't even notice that Peter was—well—at sea, so to speak."
She licked her lips and looked away. "It just didn't seem like
much of a marriage to me."

"To you? You passing judgment on the quality of a
marriage? You, the old maid schoolteacher?"

Vida straightened in her chair. Her hand went to her
hair. "I am not an old maid," she said sharply. "I am an un-
married woman. By my own choice."

"That's not the point. Even at sea, to use your metaphor,
there are moorings—promises to keep, vows to be faithful. Not
to lie and cheat and humiliate."

Vida nodded knowingly, sympathetically, and reached
again for Emily's hand. "That's it, isn't it? I mean that's what
it really is? The humiliation, that old devil pride. That's what's
so hard to take."

Emily lifted widespread fingers and looked toward the
ceiling. "I do not see," she said in carefully measured words,
"how you can sit here without any remorse at all and rational-
ize adultery. You are an adulteress, Vida Austin! The whore
of Babylon. You have coveted! You have sinned against me
and my house."

Vida rolled her eyes. "Oh, Em, don't thump the Bible at

me. You've call to be angry, yes, but not self-righteous. The good Lord sure as hell wouldn't choose you for his stone-throwing team." They stared at each other for a long hushed moment. Vida blinked first. She lowered her eyes, then looked up from under her lashes. "Emily, I am not rationalizing," she said quietly. "I'm not trying to excuse myself. I just want you to understand. I was lonely, dirt-poor-wake-up-in-the-night lonely! And Peter was lonely. It started as a friendship and it deepened and widened and became more. As long as no one was hurt we didn't see that there was any harm in it, in being a comfort to each other."

She paused thoughtfully and tilted her head to one side. Her green eyes clouded over and looked through and beyond Emily in a becalmed expression Emily had seen before, one that each time sent a bone-deep chill all the way to her feet.

"Probably," Vida said wistfully, "probably it would never have happened if Malcolm hadn't been away so much in San Francisco."

Emily's eyebrows arched into dark crescent moons. "Vida, don't do that, please," she said, drawing back in her chair. "I get very nervous when you start talking about those people."

"But it's true," Vida insisted. "It can get lonesome in a houseful of women. And when he *is* home, Momma watches us like a turkey vulture. Still! After all this time."

Emily shifted uneasily. She looked closely at Vida and took a deep breath. "Uh . . ." she began. "When did—you know, Malcolm—when did he start going to San Francisco?"

"Well now let's see. It must be six or seven years now—" She frowned. "But that's not what you're asking, is it?"

"No."

"It was two years ago when you went back to New Orleans for that reunion, that's when it started."

"I see."

"You were gone for a *month*," Vida added accusingly.

Emily leaned back and let the awful impact from the words strike her full in the chest, let her eyes watch them clutch at each other's bodies, let her ears hear their whispered endearments, their sharp animal cries. The metallic scent of sex—unmistakable—filled her nostrils.

Her breath came quickly and she turned to the typewriter. She snatched out the paper with its laughter, its labored attempts at understanding, inserted a new sheet, and typed rapidly.

"Here," she said hoarsely when she had finished. "This is what I will run next week."

Vida took the page, read it, read it again, and let it fall to the floor. "I won't do it," she said firmly. "This is my home. I won't leave here."

"I'm giving you the opportunity to resign," Emily said smoothly, suddenly quite pleased with the direction things were taking.

"Don't do this," Vida said softly. "You and I have something special, something apart and separate from Peter. You know that. We nurture each other's minds." She paused and smiled engagingly. "Why, I'm the only woman for miles around you can say Dostoevsky to and not have it taken for a sneeze."

Emily laughed in spite of herself. Vida watched her closely, waiting. "No," Emily said finally. "I'm giving you as much as I am able to, a chance to salvage what is left of your reputation."

"I won't do it."

"In that case I will tell the board to dismiss you."

"The board is happy with my work."

"Yes, of course they are. You are a superb teacher. But they will not be happy when I tell them that their vague suspicions about you are well founded, that right here, in the presence of our innocent and impressionable children, the teacher is harboring a houseful of ghosts. That you keep them in a box and let them out to materialize and have the run of the town, that your grandmother takes in sewing, your mother goes to Wednesday night prayer meetings, that there's a baby and dogs and a *goat*! I will tell them that you bed down with a spirit named Malcolm MacGuire when he isn't off in San Francisco at the opera."

The two women were quiet for a long time. They watched each other cautiously, circled each other with their eyes. Vida was the first to speak. "If you do this," she said, "if you make me leave here, I will take Peter with me."

Emily smiled. "Yes, I rather thought you would say that. But I've been thinking and I've realized that I—not Peter— am the magic ingredient in your brew. The eyes of newts and the toes of frogs and the wool from bats just don't have any flavor without the guilt from Emily. It was the guilty secret that kept the cauldron bubbling, keeping it from the valley, from Gregory, from Catherine. And oh yes, from whatshisname —Malcolm! What spice that must have added. But it was most delectable, ah yes, kept from poor old blind Emily. Well, there's no secret anymore. Take him! Go ahead and take him. I expect that even ghosts get tiresome, especially middle-aged ghosts sitting around mending nets and cursing sheep."

Vida bent forward with hunched shoulders, looking oddly frail. "Oh, Emily," she cried. "Em, what are we doing? We sit here haggling like harpies over this man. Where is the love in all of this? I loved him! You loved him, remember? And all these people he was good and kind to for all these years, they loved him." She rose to her feet, straight and tall with indignation. "We dishonor him, and ourselves, with such talk."

She bent down, picked up the sheet of paper from the floor, and thrust it into Emily's hands. "You can say that I am leaving Cadyville because of family matters." She paused and lifted her chin. "And I would be obliged if you would put in there someplace about how many of my students went on to college."

She snatched her purse from the desk and walked briskly to the door, slid its bolt, opened it wide, then turned and spoke softly. "Emily, you are a foolish woman. There are no newts' eyes or frogs' toes in this. I loved Peter and I needed him and I wanted him and I gave him no cause to doubt it, not for one moment. That's the magic, Em, that's the only magic there ever is."

Emily went to the doorway and watched as the friend of her heart, the sister of her mind, moved in tiger-bright confidence down the street toward the highway. As she crossed the square the sun caught her hair in the dappled shadows and it glistened, a golden crown. A sudden breeze swirled her skirt in folds around her and at that moment, in the shimmering waves of light meeting heat, she disappeared.

After what seemed like hours Emily closed the door and leaned stiffly against it. Except for the tick-tocking of the clock on the wall, the room was filled with silence, an oppressive, heavy hush that buzzed in her ears. She covered them with her hands and made her way with short, old woman steps back to her chair. She sat down slowly, holding herself like something easily broken. The clock ticked on and on, gathering the afternoon into its slender hands.

In the grey dimness of approaching dusk, the machine on the desk came to life and in perfect time with the beat of the clock, printed: "WHERE IS THE LOVE IN ALL OF THIS?"

Emily cried out, "Oh leave me *alone!*" Ask that fool girl, she thought. What happened to her anyway? That fool girl who wrote I love you on his chest, who burned hot and bright with the need to be filled by him—on the sand, in the redwood grove, in the orchard—flowing like a warm spring at the sight of him. Who ached for the touch, the feel, the smell, the taste of his golden body, for the sound of his wild honey words dropping on her ears, sliding over her cheeks, anointing her breasts, and coming to rest on her thighs. Who would have given her life for him because without him life was only fragments and dust and dry bowls.

It was her need—hers alone, that caused the blue heron to fly upriver to nest, caused the strawberries to put forth green-centered blossoms that turned red and sweet, caused the rain to come on a still, impotent afternoon, guided the sun across the sky and then summoned the stars. Without him, the jagged walls of green mountains that surrounded her valley could not exist, for without him, it was too painful to look upon anything so beautiful.

Where did she go? Leaving behind that dry husk of a woman who threw dirt on his grave this morning? What happened to her? That wondrous, joyous, tormented creature?

The machine clacked and clattered an instant reply: "She was never real, you know. She was his fantasy, they created her together. She was his Ondine, his Circe, his Annabel Lee. His Vida. She was his myth who lived only to receive him, to renew him, to give him life everlasting."

"Then there is no hope for us," Emily whispered. "We are lost, we are tricked. Ondine bears no children, Circe turns men into swine, Annabel Lee dies, barely a woman. And Vida! Oh dear God in heaven, *Vida Austin is mad.*"

Her words sank like pebbles thrown into the deep silent pool of the room. She listened and waited, but there were only the ripples of shadows spreading out on the bare floor. She made her stiff, cold hands into fists and struck the top of the machine. "I said that we are tricked!" she shouted.

At length the response came in labored, wounded letters. "They too are tricked. They live the trick and the myth. They are lost and there is no hope for them either. The little death they die inside the myth does not bring them everlasting life."

Emily covered her face with her hands and rocked, back and forth, back and forth, the ancient gesture. "He's gone," she said in a faint dull voice. "He is gone and I am alone and I am afraid. I am afraid of that long dark without him." She looked down at the keys, the twenty-six keys to the closets of the heart. They were wet. The heart had opened.

V<small>IRGINIA</small> M<small>AC</small>G<small>UIRE</small> — NURSE

Born 1904, Claremore, Oklahoma

"The girls no longer need me—" wrote Vida. "I congratulate myself on a job well done. They will make their mark, those two, especially Virginia who has an upright mind and the gift of healing in her hands."

CHAPTER THREE

"I HAVE A PROPOSITION TO PUT TO YOU, MISS MACGUIRE."

Virginia looked up from the appointment book. Her large hazel eyes narrowed and her cheerfully lined face assumed the tolerant expression of a woman not unaccustomed to such attention.

"Sorry, Mr. Patrick," she said, "but I don't take propositions from nine to five." She moistened her forefinger on her tongue and turned a page in the appointment book. "Besides which, it isn't ethical at any hour. Now. When does he want to see you again?"

"A week." He waited for her to look up. When she did it was with a smile, broad and friendly, to show him there were no hard feelings. "You know," he said, "under the circumstances, I can't see how the American Medical Association could object if we had a nice quiet supper and some serious business conversation."

He folded his arms on the counter and looked her straight in the eye. His light-blue shirtsleeves were rolled one turn, flaring slightly with starch and neatness, exposing forearms heavily muscled from the years of hard labor in the oil fields around Drumright. The darkened skin with its fine bleached hair came from a recent weekend of Hot Springs sun, and before that from the sun in the Bahamas. Before that, the same sun had blistered him on Wake, on Guam, and on Midway.

Virginia's hand rested on the thick chart that contained this information about Timothy S. Patrick; it also contained, as they both well knew, the results of the lymph node biopsy, a dire prognosis, and an article from the May 1946 issue of the AMA *Journal*, describing nitrogen mustard as being effective in the treatment, although not the cure, of Hodgkin's disease.

"That's not fair," she said softly.

"I don't have the time or the inclination to be fair, Miss MacGuire."

He unfolded his arms and held out his hands in a silent request for her to understand how things stood. They were, Virginia noted, large good hands like the Sunday hands of a farmer, with the callused pads and rough knuckles scrubbed, the nails cleaned deep and squarely trimmed.

He pointed a finger at the desk. "Now, I'd be much obliged if you'd just write down your address on one of those little white cards. I'll pick you up at seven o'clock and we'll have ourselves a big thick steak out at the Oil Rig."

Virginia was thoughtful for a moment, then reached for a card. On the front she wrote a date and time one week hence; on the back she wrote the number of her apartment on Riverside Drive. After he left, saluting and grinning as he went out the door, she stared down at the manila file. In it was all she had ever felt and most of what she understood. A chill passed through her; she recognized it, acknowledged it, accepted it. Virginia was that sort.

THE OIL RIG was a private club on the outskirts of Tulsa, which like all of Oklahoma—except for three-two beer—was bone dry. The bootleggers and the hard-shell Baptists kept it that way. In the public clubs which were the ones in which Virginia spent time—when she, although infrequently, spent that kind of time—you brought your own bottle of whiskey in a brown paper bag, ordered ice and mix, and on the signal from the bouncer that the sheriff's men were on their way in to take a turn of the place, you set the liquor, still in its paper sack, on the floor under the table. The money that allowed this situation to exist passed hands in the same place.

But in the private clubs, like the Oil Rig of which Timothy Patrick was a charter member, patrons kept their own personal stock behind the bar and were served from it. Or they didn't, and were served anyway. The Oil Rig and places like it were not visited by the sheriff; they consorted with higher authorities.

Tim pointed to a table in the corner, on the other side of the room from the small combo. The maître d' nodded and led them to it.

"What'll you have to drink, Miss MacGuire?"

She asked for Seven and Seven, then quickly changed her mind. "Why I think I'd like to have myself a martini if that's possible." She looked surprised and delighted by her request. "I've never had one," she explained.

He ordered a martini for her, Jack Daniels and water for himself, then laid his arm across the back of the booth and said thoughtfully, "I expect there's something about being with me that causes folks to think about what they might have missed along the way."

Virginia leaned toward him. "Mr. Patrick," she said, in a firm level voice, "for the past fifteen years I've dealt with illness. I'm accustomed to it. I'm not unsympathetic to it, mind you, but it's as much a part of my life as getting up in the morning. I couldn't do my job if I let my feelings chase me all around that office every day."

"Tim," he said.

"Virginia," she answered.

The drinks came. Tim wanted to know if the shrimp

was fresh. Yes, it had been flown in from Corpus that afternoon. He ordered the meal with the care and attention of a man investing in a work of art, consulting with her, with the waiter, with the chef who was summoned; advising, exclaiming, collaborating on a feast for all senses. To Virginia's amazement his country-boy drawl slid easily around the pronunciation of a wine born before either of them.

When the entourage had bowed and smiled and gone off with its instructions, Tim turned to Virginia and raised his glass. She lifted hers, sipped the martini, and uttered a soft hum of appreciation.

"And this," he said, "is just the beginning of the earthly delights that are in store for you."

"Are earthly delights a part of this serious business you have to discuss with me?"

"If you're the lady for the job, they sure are."

She fished out the olive and popped it in her mouth. "Okay," she said. "Shoot."

"Well, for one thing, Dr. Lukus says you're the best nurse in Tulsa County. For another, I've been watching you these last six months. I've learned a lot about you over the top edge of *National Geographic*. You're efficient, to the point, straight as a string, and you read on your lunch hour—travel folders and history books—and for the purposes of this proposition, I have concluded that you are one tough broad." He added quickly, "I mean that as the highest sort of compliment. I figure not since you were a baby has anybody called you Ginny."

She laughed. "Well, you're wrong there. Papa always called me Ginny. I was seventeen when he died." She held up her glass and peered into it. "Sure is dinky, doesn't hardly wet your whistle."

He motioned to the waiter, held up one finger, and pointed to Virginia. "I'd advise you to go easy," he laughed, "that ain't soda pop there. When you were seventeen, huh?"

She looked at him closely. "Does our business have to do with the story of my life?"

"We got to start somewhere. How'd your daddy go? He couldn't have been very old."

"Papa died of fornication," Virginia replied blandly and paused for a reaction, but Tim only nodded pleasantly and waited for her to go on. "My momma got the chronic vapors after I was born and she wasn't ever very well, although she was a damn sight weller than she let on. But I reckon that was Papa's excuse for his—let's see now, what's a nice word for it? Excesses. Yes, that'll do. My sister and I were looked after by a long string of ninnies—"

"—Nannies?" Tim questioned.

"*Nin*nies," she repeated. "You know, ninnies. And Papa humped them all."

Tim chuckled and leaned forward. "Go on."

"Then Miss Vida came and she was something else all together. Big woman! Big smile, big heart, big tits. You could tell just by looking at her that she was all appetite. Amy— that's my sis—and me, we worshiped the ground Miss Vida walked around on. And I guess—I don't really know—but I think Papa did too. I mean I don't think that what was between them was only of a carnal nature, although that certainly was a big part of it. I mean, you could *smell* that! She was with us for six years and never a day went by but what Papa spent at least a couple hours down there in her cottage. The doctor said he had a coronary, but Amy and I knew better. Malcolm MacGuire was just all fucked out."

Tim smiled. "I never heard it was an unhealthy activity."

"It is if you got to hide it. Puts an uncommon strain on the hypothalamus."

Tim's smile faded and he nodded gravely in respect for Virginia's knowledge of medical matters.

Over the salad she got through high school and four years at Stevens College in Missouri. In between bites of what she said was the best hunk of beef she had ever eaten, and then through coffee and seconds of something called a trifle—in Virginia's view the biggest culinary misnomer of all time— Tim heard about her unsuccessful attempts to get into medical school.

"My grades were good enough," she said. "Miss Vida had seen to that, but at that time it was just damn near impossible for a woman. I applied 'til I was blue in the face. Just one old fart after another wondered why I'd want to do something so unnatural. A good man and a couple of babies was all I needed to put that nonsense out of my head."

"How come you wanted to go to medical school?"

Virginia lifted her shoulders. "Well I guess Miss Vida had a part in that too. I was one of those kids who's always wagging something home and trying to fix it. If it was still breathing I figured there was hope. Miss Vida said I had the aptitude and the ability, and she could make you believe you could do anything; anything you had the guts and grit for. She used to say if you've built castles in the air, that's fine, that's where they belong. Then she'd raise her arm up like somebody leading a charge and she'd say, 'Now! Put the foundations under them.' "

"I like that," Tim said. "She make that up?"

"No. It's Thoreau. *Mister* Thoreau, she called him. You always got the feeling they were well acquainted, that he was a somebody who lived just across the way. *Any*how, I finally got tired of beating my head up against a brick wall and I came down here to Tulsa looking for "foundations." I went into nurse's training at Morningside and somehow along the way I started working as a special on critical cases. That's how I met Dr. Lukus. He watched me with patients and their families and he said he was real taken with how I could do it kindly and not get all pushed out of shape. I've been with him now for almost sixteen years. Which makes me forty-three years old in August."

She wiped her fingers on her napkin and leaned, with a great contented sigh, onto the plushness of the booth. "And that's it," she smiled. "Virginia MacGuire, soup to nuts. Not to mention two martinis. Oh my, they do oil the tongue, don't they now? And not to mention a half a bottle of—how'd you say that?"

"Caber-nay Sav-an-yon."

Virginia frowned. "Wait a minute. Didn't quite get through the nuts part. No, I am not married, never have been. Yes, I am prideful enough to say I have been asked. I fell in love once and got broken. I put myself back together with spit and chewing gum and vowed in the future I'd steer clear of that particular pot hole. No expectations, no disappointments; no promises, no sad songs. Now then, just what did you have in mind?"

What Timothy Patrick had in mind was control; as much as possible to control the course of his dying as he had the course of his life. To have a choice in the matter. That was the important thing, to make your own choices, to be responsible for and to them. Years before he had chosen to struggle to pay the back taxes on his daddy's land, even though the cash he was offered for it by Sinclair Oil caused him a delicious dizziness and thoughts of thick steaks and airplane trips to Dallas and New Orleans and—above all—a proper suit of clothes.

He chose to pay off the debt: in the daytime first, as a collar pounder then as a roustabout; at night, washing dishes and sweeping up. When it was his free and clear, he washed more dishes and swept more floors for the acreage next to his, then the next and the next, all of it, his nose told him, having buried deep in its soil that black treasure that would come up one day like flowers rushing into spring.

That's how you got to be a millionaire, he said when people asked him. "Goddamn, it's easy! You just keep on washing dishes 'til a well comes in."

What he told Virginia was, "I want to go around the world. I mean that in a sense of geography. I want to see the Tower of London and the place outside Dublin my folks came from and I want to ski in the alps if I'm up to it and see those statues in Greece and the pyramids in Egypt and I want to learn about these places as I go along. I had to leave school after the eighth grade and I feel unfinished in that respect."

"But the French," Virginia said. "Where'd you learn to speak French?"

Tim laughed. "Hell, honey, I don't speak French. I speak menu. I hired a fella, a professor, to teach me. I can read and speak menu in six languages."

Virginia smiled, completely charmed. "Go ahead."

"Well. When I get done with those places I want to go to Africa where there's just blue sky and elephants. That's where I want to cash in my chips. It's been my dream since I was a kid to see Africa. I plan to see a lot of it."

Virginia was silent. She wondered if she was hearing Irish bravado or Jack Daniels courage. Or something else. She blew out her breath slowly. "And you want me to come with you? Sort of a combination nurse and history teacher?"

"Yes, ma'am, I surely do. You know all about my condition, that it won't be easy later on. But I'll make it worth your while. I mean besides the worth of seeing all those places you read about in your travel folders. You'll be taken care of in my will, never have to lift a hand again if you're so a mind. All legal and uncontestable. My sons will sign a paper and my ex is already looked after."

Virginia narrowed her eyes. "What's the catch?"

"Well. What I need from you is your word that when you see the time has come you won't harbor any false hopes. I might, you know. It's a natural failing under the circumstances. I need your promise that you'll pull the plug without any fuss."

Virginia kept her face as smooth and expressionless as a

clock. "I think that's against the law, Timothy, even in deepest, darkest Africa."

He shook his head. "That won't be a problem. Dr. Lukus will give us a letter, then we get a permit for the medicine I have to have." He paused. "Including the morphine. All I need to know is your moral conviction on the matter."

"Well," she said slowly, drawing it out as she reached for her wine. "My moral conviction is that everybody ought to have that choice. A person's life, a person's death, those are very dear concerns."

Tim smiled with satisfaction and signaled the waiter. He ordered champagne and when it came and was bubbled out into the glasses, he raised a toast to life, death, and Virginia MacGuire.

TIM FELT FINE all the way through Ireland; so fine, in fact, that Virginia was constantly reminding him to take his iron pills and to go easier on the whiskey and heavier on the vitamins.

"Maybe I'm going to skip this month," he said. "Maybe I'm in some kind of remission they haven't written up yet."

"I think you better have the treatment anyway," said Nurse MacGuire. "It's time for it."

"First the Cheshire Cheese and the Tower of London," he said. "Then we'll talk about the treatment."

He was overdoing and Virginia knew it, but nothing in her past had prepared her for dealing with Timothy Patrick's appetite for life in the face of the loss of it. He was as difficult as a child on the mend; she earned her money.

"SAYS HERE she was executed," said Tim. "Did you know that? Pretty little thing like that?" He held out the booklet with its portrait of Anne Boleyn on the cover. "Right here on this very spot they cut off that pretty little head."

"She was five foot nine and had a big wart on her neck," said the History Teacher. "And anyhow, it served her right. She was fooling around with the king while he was still married to his first wife."

"That so?"

Virginia's face was full of disapproval. "You see, the old queen, Katharine, had one little girl and a batch of miscarriages. Then Henry went sniffing after Anne there, but she wouldn't have him unless he married her. So he dumped Katharine, saying it was because their marriage wasn't legal and anyhow she hadn't given England an heir." She paused and pulled a disgusted face. "Then I declare if Anne didn't do the same damn thing. Had a baby girl and miscarried a boy. By that time old Henry got the itchy balls again so he dumped Anne, accused her of being in the bushes with five different guys, including her own brother. She was convicted and . . ." Virginia clicked her tongue and drew her finger across her throat."

Tim winced. "That's real unfair."

"Poetic justice, I'd say."

"A mite harsh, I'd say." He was looking at the portrait.

Virginia laughed. "Well, my sympathies are with the old lady, poor soul. She wrote Henry a love letter when she was dying in exile where the squirrely old bastard sent her, signed it Katharine the Queen. Now that's style!"

Tim stretched out his arms as if to measure the small fenced plot where Anne Boleyn was buried. "Five *nine*?"

Virginia raised her eyebrows. "She's holding her pretty little head."

Tim shuddered, took one last forlorn look at the plot, then wandered off to shoot yet more pictures of the courtyard.

Virginia sat down on a bench to wait for him and to sort through the travel folders she carried in her bag. When he returned his face was flushed, his eyes unnaturally bright. She stood up quickly and touched his shoulder. "You have a fever, Timothy," she said. "Come on, let's go back to the hotel."

HE COULD HAVE taken the injection in smaller amounts over a four-day period but he chose to have the full dose at one time —along with the full effects of nausea and fits of vomiting— to get it over with. This way he lost only two or three days to the bed, rather than five or six. Those days that he himself saved were precious to him and he spent them even more lavishly than the others.

Three days after the treatment, Tim announced that he was fit and ready to push on. He thought it might be sort of a lark to go to that place in France where they did all the miracles. Not that he expected any for himself mind you, but he surely did not want to pass up any possibilities.

"Are you religious, Timothy?" Virginia asked him.

"Well. You know what they say. Nobody ever dies an atheist."

Actually, Virginia thought Lourdes was a fine idea. There were hotels there that dealt in health and piety; in nutritious meals and baths and abstinence; all of which could not but help a body that had spent two weeks celebrating its return to the old sod, and another in sampling the pubs of the old enemy.

TIM WAS SOLEMN and drawn tightly into himself as they walked toward the sacred grotto.

"Bernadette was fourteen when she started seeing the visions," Virginia was saying. "She saw the Virgin Mary eighteen times in this place where they put up the statue." She peered up at him. "Are you listening? Are you listening to the history lesson?"

"God! Look at them! Look at the canes and the crutches and the wheelchairs! I had no idea there were so many folks so bad off."

In the grotto they watched as a woman knelt before the Blessed Mother and a few moments later came bounding to her feet, clasping her hands to a face filled with intense light. She crossed herself and walked, in a kind of majesty, away from the shrine, leaving two crutches at the Virgin's feet.

"Hysteria, most likely," Virginia whispered to Tim.

"Bullshit? Is that what you're saying?"

"No. Not necessarily. There are probably a lot of people cured here. But chances are, a lot of them didn't have anything physically wrong to begin with."

"You mean being crippled can be in your mind?"

Virginia smiled. "Well. Sort of. But it can be just as real."

Tim shook his head sadly and turned to leave. "Let's go see the fortress, Virginia. Okay? What they're selling here is hope and I've not got the price."

He moved away. Virginia lingered, wishing she could somehow close in on the miracle, wishing for the first time in her life that she had learned how to pray.

IT WAS IN ROME, standing in the center of the crumbling splendor of the Coliseum, that he commenced calling her Ginny.

"It's damp here, Timothy," she said. "We shouldn't stay. The dampness isn't good for you." She tugged on his arm but he didn't move, didn't seem to hear her. He was listening to Titus Caesar open the games that would last for a hundred days, to the roar of pleasure that went up as ships sailed by in a flooded arena, to the chariots thunder through the arches, to the lightning crash against the walls, to the rumbling earth crack the great pillars and finally, to the whine of U.S. bombs as they fell.

"Listen," he said. "Listen! Do you hear it?"

"What, Timothy? What is it?"

"Time, Ginny," he whispered. "Time," and he reached for her hand.

Later at the hotel the moon shone in pale kindness across the bed and both of them believed for one full night that they were as young and as sound as they used to be.

IN A VILLAGE high in the mountains on Crete, Tim spent six days in a racking, punishing, delayed reaction to the latest treatment. Bone marrow depression was an expected side effect of nitrogen mustard, but this anemia was so severe Virginia sought out the doctor in the village to find out if a transfusion could be arranged. He prescribed penicillin instead, for the respiratory infection which, he said, was draining the patient's strength and slowing his recovery. For the primary illness, he advised more iron and more rest; much rest was needed in these cases.

On the morning of the tenth day there was color in Tim's face; real color, not ragged fever patches on his cheeks. He announced in a shaky voice that he would bathe, shave, and dress and that they would have a big breakfast at the cafe in the square.

"You will stay right here and have your breakfast out on the balcony," she said. "I've already sent for it."

"You're bossy," he grumbled.

"I am, as you said, one tough broad, and I'm in charge of your activities that affect your health. It's kinda like being in charge of the wind."

He leered at her playfully and patted the side of the bed.

"You crazy Okie, that's just exactly what I'm saying. You're not up to that just yet."

"But I will be. Maybe we could just go over the preliminaries so's I won't forget how. By the time we get to Nairobi I'll be fit for an orgy."

She bit into her lip and turned her face away from him. Not Africa. Not yet.

"Ginny?"

"Yes, Timothy."

"You gave your word. You promised."

THEY KEPT A ROOM at the Fairview Hotel in Nairobi, to which they would return when Virginia saw signs of overfatigue or a prolonged reaction to the treatment. On three occasions he had blood transfusions for the anemia, but for the most part and owing to Virginia's fierce vigilance, the disease was kept under reasonable control.

They located a British pilot for hire and retained him on a standby basis to fly them to those places where Tim wanted to go, and where by other outlandishly expensive arrangements, a camp would be set up and ready for them when they arrived.

Tim became expert with both the Graphex that he would mount on a tripod and the Leica, ever present around his neck. He would spend hours with the big Graphex set up in a blind constructed for him by beaters and "boys" who usually hired out on hunting safaris and who laughed and shook their heads at the American's puny weapon. Virginia, like an overprotective mother, told them haughtily that the Bwana captured the spirit of the animal in the black box and that this required stronger magic than merely killing it.

One afternoon she sat waiting for him to return to their tent on the Uaso Nyiro where they had camped for nearly three symptom-free weeks. He had gone off to look for the martial eagle again. That morning he had said he would not be back until he found it and—he added, grinning at Virginia

—had captured its spirit in his black box. A book lay on its back beside Virginia and her mind was empty of all but the sounds around her; of the river moving and of wings brushing the air in sudden flight. Her companions were three vervet monkeys, begging with the arrogance of the deserving, and a dozen solemn marabou storks in formal attire. The storks jousted with each other with loud bill-clapping for the leftovers of a crocodile feed. On the sandbar across the river, two baboon troops came to drink and to argue over boundaries. The bill-clapping of the storks seemed elegant by comparison.

Earlier, Joseph, their all-purpose camp manager, had given her the daily Swahili lesson and gone off to gather a certain kind of wild lettuce and certain herbs which he would later prepare in a certain way—part of their unspoken agreement to make the Bwana's blood strong. Joseph came from a farming area near Narok where there was, he said, no work. He raised plenty of food and had a grand house. He waved his hand contemptuously at the circle of tents. His house had wooden walls and a fine tin roof on which the rain sang. But King George said the children—there were nine of them— must have special clothing for school and in order to buy these many trousers and shirts and dresses, Joseph worked for the Americans and the Europeans who came to Kenya to shoot animals and live in these poor cloth tents.

One of the vervets screamed and Joseph, his big teeth gleaming in his blue-black face, emerged from the forest carrying a large basket. He winked at Virginia. "For tea," he said. "Tea? You remember how to say?"

She thought for a moment. Timothy was much better at this than she. "Now you just hold your horses there, Joseph. I'm thinking. Ah . . . *chui*?"

Joseph pretended dismay then laughed and slapped his bare thigh. "*Eee!* That leopard, Missy Bwana. *Chai. Chai* be tea."

She squeezed her eyes shut and repeated it dutifully, then they both turned at the sound of a motor in the distance.

When the Land Rover came to a stop, Tim climbed out slowly, holding onto the windshield and then the fender with both hands. He took a deep breath and walked with short, dragging steps toward the tent, his back held rigid and askew. The disease, which could visit any organ at will, could swell the liver or the spleen, could close the bronchus and cut off the breath, or block the ureters and cause the kidneys to fail, had instead settled for and in Tim's backbone, causing the faulty vertebrae to clamp down on nerve roots and produce shooting stars of white pain.

He didn't notice her, she knew that. If he had seen her he would have rearranged his face into a concealing smile. Joseph stepped to the side and Virginia moved back quickly so it would appear she had just come out of the tent. "Hi, sugar!" she called, playing his game, then she ducked back inside and came out holding a bottle of Jack Daniels and two glasses overhead. It was, this whiskey, the treatment of choice.

That night she casually suggested a quick trip to Nairobi and a check-in for a couple of days at the hospital. Maybe another transfusion. Couldn't hurt.

"No," he said firmly. "I want to go back to the Mara for the migration. Joseph says there are wildebeest and zebra by the thousands."

"But it'll soon be time for the rains, Timothy. I don't think—" The words trailed off as she looked into his face, waxen and drawn in the light from the fire. "Sure," she said cheerfully, "I'd like to be there for the migration. I'll tell Joseph and we'll plan to leave in a couple days."

When they had been only fond of one another they had been honest. Now that they were in love, they lied constantly.

WILDEBEEST PASSED in an unbroken line, following an ancient path on the other side of the river from the camp in the Mara.

It was a cycle that never began and never ended, but simply paused while the grass died in one place and grew in another. Young wildebeest were taken by lions and hunting dogs along the way; old wildebeest died of time and small miscalculations. Always others took their places in the lines.

One afternoon, Tim and Virginia tired of wildebeest watching and drove out onto the savannah to see topi at a mud wallow. The animals churned up the mud with their hooves, then knelt and twisted their necks so that the horns dug into the mud and came up coated and dripping with it. They lined up for this curious ritual, each one politely waiting its turn.

"So civilized," Virginia laughed. "They must be British."

Tim snorted. "Civilized! Civilized folks don't chop the heads off their queens."

Virginia laughed again and squeezed his arm. "I do believe that you are a bit smitten with Anne Boleyn."

"Well, I don't understand why you're so hard on her. Your Miss Vida, you said she was fooling around with your daddy, but you're not mad at her. And that little English girl, you said she got what she deserved. Seems to me that Anne and Vida had a sin in common."

"Well of course they did, Timothy. I never said they didn't. But I *loved* Miss Vida. People you love don't sin, they just show poor judgment from time to time."

AFTER A FEW WEEKS the whiskey stopped working. It took too much of it to dull the pain and Tim refused to end his days as a falling-down drunk. So now, for the first time since she had packed her black bag with all the necessary and anticipated medications, Virginia lifted out the false bottom and removed the morphine. She did not tell Tim; instead she said it would be more effective if he got his B-12 by injection rather than by mouth. He had no choice but to believe her.

The thunder came as if summoned at five-thirty each evening and then the warm rain followed. Tim would sleep and Virginia would sit like a guard dog under the overhead flap of canvas in front of the tent. One evening just as the storm was moving on, Joseph appeared with a new brew of tea. He hung around for a while, grunting and clearing his throat. She waited, as was their custom, for him to speak when he was ready. Finally he told her that there was an old man in Narok—not far—who had strong spells for the evil spirits that lived in the body.

She told him sharply that she would not waste the Bwana's money on the likes of witch doctors. Plants and herbs were old and respected remedies, but magic spells were for fools. She was, after all, a registered nurse and of a scientific bent. But that night Tim cried out in his sleep each time he moved and the next morning Virginia asked Joseph, who allowed himself to accept her apology, to take her to Narok—to take her to the old man.

Narok was poor and ugly; the old man's house crouched like a toad in the center of town, its steps and sagging porch red with road dust. Joseph went ahead to announce her needs and plead her worthiness. Moments later she was shown into a small garden behind the house which was cool and quiet and bloomed with the surprise of red and yellow flowers.

The old man smiled and nodded, then indicated with a graceful sweep of his arm that she was to sit on a low flat rock. He sank down on the ground opposite her, narrowing his eyes and pulling deeply on a long thin pipe. With a tilt of his head he gave her to understand that she might speak.

"Joseph says that you are a great doctor with strong medicine," she began. She was always struck with how formal her speech became when she talked with the people of this country, of how in awe she was of their great dignity. "My—" she paused. How should she describe him? Her employer? Her patient? Her beloved?

The old man pursed his lips. "The Bwana. Yes?"

"He has a very bad sickness. Swelling here—" She touched her neck on either side at the back of her jaw. "And here—" she added, placing her knuckles under her armpits. "Where the white blood is carried. You know?" He nodded and Virginia suddenly felt very foolish. How *could* he know?

"He is pale?" the old man asked. "More and more weak?"

"Yes," she answered quickly. "Anemia."

"From lack of iron?"

"No. I give him iron three times a day. It is from the treatment he takes for the sickness."

The old man rubbed his chin thoughtfully. "There is a failure of marrow formation?"

Virginia looked at him sharply, at his half-naked body with its ornamental scars. "Yes, doctor," she said slowly. "That is correct."

He shrugged. "He can be transfused."

"Yes, he has. Many times. He doesn't want that anymore. And he is in great pain, the bones in his back are—" She leaned forward. "Joseph says you have powerful medicine. Can you help him?"

"I can ease his pain."

"I can do *that*," Virginia said. "I'm giving him morphine."

"Joseph says your friend has been sick a long time. Joseph says your friend came to the Mara to die."

Virginia looked away.

"You nurse him?"

"Yes."

"You force him to live?"

"I *love* him."

The old man sighed and pulled on his pipe.

"There must be something!" Virginia insisted. "Aren't there herbs, aren't there plants? Aren't there—?" She drew a deep breath. "Aren't there spells?"

The old man chuckled. "I'm a physician, Missy Bwana,

not a *mundunugu*. I practiced for many years at the hospital in Mombasa."

"But Joseph said—"

"Of course Joseph said. I have magic for my patients here. I use it because they believe in it. Belief itself is the cure for many disorders." He paused. "If I make a spell for this man you love, will he believe it will make him well?"

Virginia thought of Lourdes and the crutches at the feet of the Virgin. She covered her face with her hands. "No," she said, her voice muffled and small, and when she uncovered her face it was wet from her tears. "But I will," she whispered, "I will believe."

He looked at her kindly, shaking his head. "Joseph can do as much with his herbs as I can with mine." He rose and touched her shoulder. "I am so very sorry."

AS THE DAYS crept by Tim spent more and more time on his cot, floating through the hours. When the morphine would begin to wear off, Virginia would appear, hypodermic in hand to give him his "vitamins" and a glass of Joseph's tea. Tim would obediently hold out his arm and gaze at her in sad and silent rebuke as she emptied the needle and made crisp, nursely sounds. They no longer spoke of promises.

In the mornings Joseph would move the cot out in front of the tent where Tim would watch the dwindling trek of wildebeest and on occasion, when he felt up to it, capture the spirit of the mongoose that came for handouts. After lunch Joseph would move the cot back inside, then he and Virginia would support Tim between them into the tent where he would sleep, Virginia out front reading in the canvas chair.

On one such afternoon Virginia suddenly screamed for Joseph who came running. She pointed to the other side of the river where a lone hyena had attacked a bull wildebeest. She paced up and down the bank, shaking her fist, shivering in outrage. "There's just one of the bastards! Look, Joseph! He's just standing there. Why doesn't he run? Oh, Joseph, why doesn't he *fight?*"

Joseph turned his smooth, impassive face from her to the scene on the other side. As they watched, the big bull sank down into the tall savannah grass. Joseph shrugged. "Old maybe. Maybe sick." He listened for a moment then shook his head sadly. "He unlucky. Much better Simba find you at the end. That one bad killer—*eee*—very slow."

That evening Virginia dressed in the bright Somali caftan Tim had bought for her in Nairobi, pinned a red flower in her hair, made martinis which she tried to cool in the river, and fussed over the table Joseph had set by the fire.

"We're celebrating how chipper you look," she said in answer to the question in Tim's eyes as they took in her dress and the table with its crisp linen and bouquet of flowers. "Your color is much better," she went on, "and I think you're putting on some weight." She poked at him playfully. "Course a lot of it's around the middle. Joseph and I are at it about who gets the credit. He says it's the new tea but I know damn well it's the vitamins. Whatever—I think we've found the formula."

Tim responded to her airy chatter by laughing out loud over the tepid martinis and bringing an appetite, spare but game, to the table.

Later when he'd settled onto the cot and held out his arm she went over it all again—the color, the weight, the vitamins —all the while bustling about. "I'm adding extra C to the B-12," she said. "I'm sure that's what's making such a difference."

He nodded sleepily and she sat down on the edge of the cot, kissed him first on his lips and then on his forehead, smoothed his hair and ran her finger down his cheek, then began to talk about the martial eagle Joseph had seen just a mile or so downriver.

"In a couple of days, maybe you'll be able to go look for it. Oh but now—now Timothy, we need our sleep."

He nodded, smiled, and closed his eyes while she gave him the injection. And then Virginia MacGuire—one tough broad—moved to the chair by the side of the cot, took his hand in hers, and waited for his heart to stop.

Elizabeth Austin — Spinster

Born 1891, Robina County, Oklahoma

Aunt Vida often said, with a deliciously wicked chuckle, that she and Elizabeth scared the living daylights out of the few men who got up the necessary gumption to come calling. This was due partly to Elizabeth's tongue which, according to Vida, was sharpened every morning before breakfast on the whetstone, and suffered neither the foolish nor the ineptly well-meaning.

CHAPTER FOUR

Elizabeth Austin, the tenant in 201, was startled by the sound of the buzzer. It had not rung since a month before when a bill collector came to the wrong apartment, and weeks before that when the gas man—new to the route—had asked for directions to the meter and was given them, finally, suspiciously, through a modest crack in the peephole. She approached the door with soft-soled caution, unhooked the small wooden window, opened it very slowly, and peered into the hallway, blinking like a nocturnal animal suddenly thrust into the light.

It was the boy from the third floor, the one whose mother often came in late at night, her high-heeled footsteps at times accompanied by heavy, impatient ones that caused the stairs to creak and moan with complaints of age.

"What do you want?" she demanded, cross with the child for the turn he had given her.

He lifted his face at the sound of her voice, and strained to see past the small, heavy screen. When she had moved here from the farm twenty years before, Elizabeth had paid out two whole dollars to have the sight-hole cut into the door and the double screen attached. Through it she guarded her fortress and kept the world at bay.

"Well, what is it? What do you want, boy?"

Without answering, he held up to the screen a sparrow, its neck and breast uneven patches of down and skin, its beak open in a silent cry.

She hesitated, then reluctantly drew the bolt and stretched her thin, flabby arm to undo the chain at the top. Inch by inch she opened the door.

"He was sitting on the sidewalk," the boy explained. "I couldn't find no nest." He held the bird out to her, his palm open, his arm stiff and raised from the shoulder. "I guess his momma's gone off."

Elizabeth took a step backward into the room. She spoke defensively. "I can't do anything about it. Why did you bring it to me?"

He took a step forward. "You had a bird before," he said. "I seen it in the window lots of times."

"That was different," she said quickly. "That was a canary, a tame bird. This one's wild."

"Can't you just keep him tonight?" the boy asked. "Maybe he'll be all better in the morning."

Elizabeth sighed and her mind was suddenly crowded with all the creatures the girl she had been had hoped would be better in the morning. In her fifty-nine years she had learned, learned all too well, that the morning more often took than gave. She sighed again. "Oh well," she said, "what can it matter."

She took the grey heap of feathers and curled her hand around them, watching with satisfaction as the talons clutched weakly at her third finger, bent in toward her palm to make a perch.

"Likely, it'll not last the night," she warned the boy. "You mustn't hold any hope."

He looked up at her with wide, worried eyes. "It won't hurt none, will it?" he asked.

"What won't hurt?"

"It won't hurt his chances none if I hope?"

Elizabeth came close to smiling, but decided against it. "Come along," she said and led the way briskly, purposefully to the kitchen, forgetting to latch and lock and bolt and otherwise secure the door.

"Here now," she said. "You hold it while I fix it something to eat. No, no, not like that. Bend your finger in so it'll have some support, a place to put its feet. Creatures need to know where their feet are."

She filled a saucepan with water from the tap and set it on the burner. From the refrigerator she took bread, an egg, and a small can of evaporated milk. "The egg's for later," she said, "but only the yolk," and she eased it into the water. She tore a piece of bread into minute shreds and moistened them with milk. "I'll take the bird now," she said. "You climb up on that stool there and get me that box of toothpicks from the third shelf."

The boy did as he was told while Elizabeth carried the bird and the bowl of wet crumbs to the table. At the mere whisper of a touch on the side of the beak, it opened in a yellow-ringed pink gape. Elizabeth took a toothpick. The boy watched with rapt attention as she dipped the rounded end of it into the lumpy gruel, then gasped as he saw it disappear deep into the bird's throat. Elizabeth repeated this motion several times, until the bird no longer gulped and stretched its wobbly head up for more.

"He sure was hungry all right," the boy observed happily. "He sure can put it away."

Elizabeth glanced at him from the corner of her eye. His hair, matted and musty smelling, covered his ears and the back of his neck, and fell in greasy tendrils over his unwashed face. Nine? Ten? Maybe eleven? Well, for goodness sakes she could ask—no harm in that. No. She would not ask. One innocent question could cause the mouth to run away with itself, could cause you to learn much more than you ever wanted to know.

It was better not to ask; speculation was safer. He was bone skinny, that was for sure, his elbows poking sharply through the holes of a faded shirt that plainly had not been bought with him in mind.

"And how about you?" she said. "You had your supper?"

He nodded quickly that he had, and she knew he lied. Even so she regretted her words, regretted the little piece of freedom they took from her. For twenty years she had successfully avoided lifting a hand to do for anyone. And no one had done for her. She was financially and emotionally solvent. She had a small income from the cautious investment of her share of the profit from the sale of the old home place. Letters and Christmas cards from her sisters and brothers had gone unanswered until they were no longer sent. No family, no friends, no obligations. No one to mourn, no one to be mourned by. The way she wanted it. Twenty years in the same building and she still offered only curt nods to the other occupants. The way she wanted it. She closed her eyes to the poverty, the neglect that thrived in the neighborhood, nourishing her isolation with her own well-washed three rooms, her frugally but properly fed body, her careful attention to the maintenance of solitude.

"How come he's all stuck out on one side?" the boy wanted to know.

"That's its crop," she answered. "It works something like your stomach. It'll go down soon; a bird digests its food very quickly. In an hour it'll be hungry again."

"How come you know about birds?"

"You're just full of how-comes, aren't you?"

The boy pulled back into himself and almost disappeared in the shirt.

Elizabeth sighed. "I was raised up on a farm. You learn to doctor animals. And people too for that matter. You learn to do for yourself. It's a hard kind of life."

The boy accepted this information gravely, then looked around the room as if wondering what to do next, his eyes lingering for just a moment on the loaf of bread on the counter.

Freedom and solitude aside, once someone had contrived to get past her front door, Elizabeth felt bound by common courtesy and moral duty to see to it they were fed. "You can wash your hands there in the sink," she said. "There's lunch meat and mayonnaise and sweet pickles in the icebox." She pointed to the loaf of bread, and set out a plate and a knife. "I'd be pleased if you would help yourself while I find a shoe box for this bird."

By the end of the week the bird was able to hop up on the side of the shoe box and there, clutching the edge, demand in a lusty squawk to be fed. Elizabeth no longer used the toothpick but held out tiny pieces of ground sirloin, a heretofore unthought-of luxury, alternated with slivers of peeled apple, to him on her forefinger.

"What'll we call him?" the boy asked one afternoon, chewing noisily on the apple he shared with the bird.

"We'll not call him anything," she answered firmly. "We had a saying in the Austin family, 'When you name a thing you mean to keep it.' We named our milk cows, the mules, the old sow, the laying chickens, but everything that was to become food or be turned loose went nameless. This bird will soon be ready to go, to fly away and do for itself."

The boy opened his mouth to speak but seemed to think better of it.

"Now I told you the night you brought him here that he was wild," she reminded him.

"But he's tame now," the boy mumbled, ducking his head. And the bird, as if to prove the truth of the boy's words, hunkered down on its feet and with a triumphant cry, flew to Elizabeth's shoulder.

The boy giggled and took a tissue from the box on the counter. "He shit on you, Miss Austin," he said, and handed her the tissue.

"He made waste," she corrected him as she took the bird from her shoulder and returned it to the shoe box. It pecked at her finger and made a curious deep sound in its throat, a new sound, like singing. "He'll soon be ready to go," she said. "We must get him some seed and let him eat by himself."

"What's he doing now?"

"That's called grooming or preening. That's how he keeps himself clean, running his beak over his feathers. After all, he doesn't have the advantage of a bathtub and soap and hot water like we do."

The next day when the boy appeared at her door, his hair was washed and slicked back and he was wearing a clean shirt.

AS MUCH AS daily rising at six and retiring at ten in the evening; as much as twice weekly trips to the grocer's; as much as Wednesday night to church and Friday morning to the lending library; as much as these, loneliness had become a habit with Elizabeth and she found it the most difficult aspect of her well-ordered life to change. She adjusted quickly to, and indeed benefited from, her morning walks to the butcher's for a pinch of fresh ground meat. She found that a book selected in fifteen minutes' time could be just as rewarding or just as disappointing as one pondered over for more than an hour. As for the Wednesday night services, she was again one of God's shepherds caring for one of His creatures, and so was closer to the Father in her own house than in His.

Hers was the dawn-to-dusk day of the bird and the visits of the boy, and more often than not, in the fine mist of pleasure they brought to her, she would forget to stretch her thin body with its papery, blue-veined arms to slip the chain into place. Elizabeth felt herself filling up; it frightened her.

AS HE GREW OLDER the bird spoke the three languages: the arrogant chirp of hunger; the soft wail of affection when he settled into the evening of Elizabeth's unpinned hair; and the last, the least often heard, the deep trill at once joyous and melancholy that touched a place in Elizabeth's heart unused since she was a girl.

"Is he scared when he sounds like that?" the boy asked.

"No, I don't think so," Elizabeth answered, but her tone was doubtful. "I think," she went on, "that it comes to him that he's a winged thing and he's a little startled by it."

The boy looked puzzled. "I thought maybe it was 'cause all of a sudden he missed his momma."

Elizabeth's face took on its no-nonsense expression. "*We're* his momma," she said. "We look after him properly; we do right by him. That's more than most of us ever get."

"Did you have a momma?"

"I have never known a child to ask so many personal questions," she said impatiently. Then she smiled, not broadly, but it was recognizable as a smile. "Yes, I had a momma. She died when I was a girl and then *I* became the momma. It's the responsibility of the oldest, but my sister Vida was always one to do as she pleased. You could say she flew off, so the duty came to me. I looked after them 'til they all went away, one by one, then I looked after my papa 'til he passed on." She glanced at the boy over her glasses and said evenly, "I told you, it's a hard life."

The boy nodded, then took a deep breath. "My momma told me to ask you something."

"What's that?"

"If I could stay here nights on the weekend for a while. She says I'm here so much anyway she figures you won't mind." Elizabeth tilted her head and turned her ear toward him as if she hadn't quite heard. "She'll pay for my meals," he said quickly. "She's got this new job and she'll be working nights on the weekends."

Elizabeth pulled her lips into a thin line. Of *course* she would not say that had been her impression all along—the oldest night work there was. "For how long would that be, do you suppose?"

"I don't know. Momma says she's working double shifts so she can save up enough to get us out to California. She says there's a whole lot of money to be made out in California."

"I'm sure that's so," said Elizabeth. She would *not* ask— there was no way in this world that she would ask—wild horses could not force her to ask this child about the where-abouts of his daddy.

But her thoughts were so restless and agitated, the boy got the gist of them. "My daddy didn't come back from the war. He was killed someplace in France. I can't say the place but I can write it down if you want me to."

"I'm sorry."

"I had a daddy."

"Well, of course you did! Who ever said you didn't!" She sighed. "Yes, you tell your momma it's just fine for you to stay. Now then, I've made a pot of split pea soup and a fresh peach cobbler. You wash your hands and face while I dish it up."

THE BOY would come directly to Elizabeth's from school, which he was now attending five full days a week.

"No school—no bird," said Elizabeth. And he could spend time with the bird only after he had finished his home-work, after she had checked it to see that it was correctly and neatly done.

On the weekends he would spend the night on Eliza-beth's divan, where he would sleep between starched and ironed sheets. He was often kept awake by the wonder of such luxury.

THE BIRD'S "WASTE," as Elizabeth called it in her tight-lipped way, was a challenge to her housekeeper's soul. Uncaged, it had free flight of the flat, and its droppings were numerous.

"Now, Bird—" she scolded, dabbing at the small black and white puddles with endless tissues, and she realized that from "it" had come "he" and from "he" had come "Bird" and with that, the acknowledgment of a special destiny. She had named the thing, and now she had to deal with it.

"He's not really ready yet," she would say when the boy questioned her. "We'll worry about that when the time comes."

Elizabeth took comfort from her words, but for the boy they were the familiar sounds of the unknown. When? What? Why? And the answers, the vague, grownup answers. Well, It Depends. Well, We'll See. Well, It Will All Work Out.

Without realizing it, without meaning to—meaning to do just the opposite—the boy forced Elizabeth to keep what she regarded as her solemn word, to fulfill what she believed was her responsibility to the Balance of Nature and to God.

The nails were rusted in place, their heads fragile with age and weather, and they resisted the claw of the hammer with which the boy tried to remove them.

"Why did you nail down the hook?" he asked, as one nail crumbled into red bits.

"So no one could get in," Elizabeth answered.

"How could anyone get in?" he asked, with some impatience. "This is the second floor."

She looked over his shoulder. "Can you open it now?"

In answer he banged against the hook with the hammer; it gave and he pushed at the screen which foundered in the air, creaking on its upper supports. Leaning out, he lifted it up then down, and turning it sideways, eased it inside.

"Okay," he said in a flat voice, and shoving his hands into his pockets, walked away from her.

"Bird?" she called, her tone breathy and high-pitched, trying to convey to the boy a sense of fine adventure. "Come see the world, Bird!"

The sparrow, now sleek and beautiful with the full markings of the male, flew from the yellowed shade of the floor lamp to Elizabeth's head and pulled at strands of hair.

"We'll just sit here quietly," she said, keeping her head perfectly still while she settled into a chair. "We'll let him discover his freedom for himself."

The boy turned swiftly and spoke in anger. "He'll die if you let him go."

"He'll die if I keep him," she answered quietly.

"You just don't want the bother!" he flung at her. "You just don't want to look after him anymore."

Elizabeth closed her eyes. How could she explain? How could she explain that it was not the bother, but the worry. The worry and the pity, the burdens of affection. How could she explain what she herself did not understand.

The bird flew to the floor, stretched his body, and looked with interested cockings of his head at the window, and after a long moment, hopped delicately across the worn roses in the rug, crouched, and flew to the sill. He pecked at the nail shavings and the peeling paint. As they watched he made the sound, half wild, half sweet music, in his throat and like a thought not fully realized, was gone. Elizabeth sat quite still, her thin hips, her straight back pushed against the chair, her eyes moving from the boy to the window, empty of all but sky, and back again.

Then, as suddenly as he had flown the bird reappeared, commencing at once to peck at the window, and then to groom himself, spreading his wings and running his beak quickly over each feather.

Elizabeth reached out her hand and the preening stopped. "Bird?" she called softly. He crouched, drew himself in, and became very small. "Bird?" she whispered again. He fluttered once in the old way, then took flight.

They waited for a long time, not speaking, pretending to each other that they did not wait. After dusk—the time of roosting—had crept in, then out of the room, the boy went to the window and put the screen back in place. He hooked it, pounded a nail over it, and was gone, as quietly and as finally as the bird.

After a time, Elizabeth switched on the floor lamp and heavily, her body stiff with the silence it had endured, went to the door, locked it, and slid the chain into place.

CATHERINE VALENTINE—HOUSEWIFE

Born 1913, Cadyville, California

In spite of her numerous obligations and hectic schedule, Emily never missed a parent-teacher conference with Vida, during which time she could be counted on to commit the sin of pride regarding her son, Gregory, and the sin of anger regarding her daughter, Catherine.

CHAPTER FIVE

HE ANNOUNCED IT GRAVELY. There were black specks in her aura. She had a need for more protein and more vitamins; probably—from the texture of the dark areas—C and A in particular.

"What did you have for breakfast?"

"Coffee," Catherine replied, as if admitting to a misdemeanor. "And cigarettes."

"Is that your usual pattern?"

There did not seem to be the quality of judgment in his voice; it was, then, simply an inquiry. "Well. Yes," she said, and after a significant pause, added, "lately."

Of course she needed protein, she knew *that*. There was a full-length mirror on her bathroom door and another in the hallway. Both advised that her clothes hung on her like so much summer wash on the line, not even clipped down with pins but thrown over the wire and ready to be blown away on the first breeze. She knew that! And that her eyes stared back at her, hollow and glazed out of a face fast turning the color of rising bread. She wanted to know from him what she did *not* know: what he could see that she could not.

She had come because Professor Scarlatti had been recommended with awe and reverence by Caroline, her next-door neighbor who was knowledgeable in all things. "He sees right through your skin," Caroline had whispered in wonder. "Right into your head. Right into your very soul!"

But here he was with the protein and the vitamins, going on and endlessly on about these little black specks that surrounded her.

"Isn't there anything else?" she asked hesitantly. "Can you see anything else around me?"

He smiled in a fatherly way. "Is there something in particular you wish me to look for?"

She sighed. "Well, you know. What's going to happen?"

He shut his eyes tight so that the skin on the bridge of his nose crinkled up under his glasses and the edges of his cheeks made deep troughs that could hold tears.

"A*ha*," he said, "you wish to know about the job . . ." He paused, squinted at her. "No. No, it's the children," he amended quickly. "You have children." It was almost but not quite a question.

Yes. She had children. She had not given them a good solid thought—or meal either, for that matter—in weeks; six weeks to the day. But she did have children. Max was at an age where he welcomed parental neglect; it was Becky who suffered the loss. She tiptoed around the far reaches of her mother's days and nights, signaling silent, round-eyed questions, being cautious as she awkwardly smoothed her lumpy bed, tucked in trailing sheets, washed her own clothes when no clean blouses appeared in her closet, made peanut butter sandwiches, stuffing them into brown paper bags, quietly requesting change for milk, then hanging around in the driveway, straddling her bicycle, waiting for the reminder to be careful.

She nodded that yes she had children.

The professor squeezed up his eyes again. "I see," he said in a low, solemn voice. "It is, then, the man."

Catherine leaned far forward and breathed out her relief.

"Basically, you need more protein," he insisted. "You

have a lot of energy loss right now which is indicative of a low blood sugar. In other words, we have to get the blood sugar up and bring you into a more stable condition. When do you normally eat?"

"In the afternoon," she said flatly. "Then something, a bowl of soup or something before bed." Maybe this was all preliminary stuff that had to be got out of the way before they could get on to the important question. That question being the rest of her life.

"Just alter your pattern a little," he said, emphasizing his instruction with a kindly tilt of his head and widespread fingers. "Have some fruit juice and a hard-boiled egg in the mornings. It will help to stabilize your condition—your physical condition. You see, you have too many dark areas around you. Basically, that's indicative of too much energy loss. Have you ever been anemic?"

She shook her head that she hadn't. For this she could have gone to the *doctor*! It would have been cheaper.

"More tired now than before? Do you feel tired?"

"I am de*pressed*," she said sullenly.

"Well, that I understand. I'll talk about that later. But basically if you want to stablize your depression it would be wise to keep the blood sugar high. You should be eating a little something four times a day, getting protein into you. It will affect your mental outlook."

She nodded again and peered at him to determine whether he was finished with all that sort of thing.

He wasn't. "Watch through at least April of next year as far as your diet is concerned." He looked beyond and around her while he spoke, at her aura she supposed, as she tried to move her eyes into his line of vision. "You will find that this period between now and April is one where there's fluctuation mentally and emotionally, and in order to keep reasonably stable you want to have as many things going well as possible —your physical health being one of them."

Catherine drummed the sides of the chair with her broken

fingernails. Into her very soul, indeed! The man was a charlatan; Caroline was a fool!

"Basically," he said, "I'm going to be talking to you about the two yous—the inner, that's the spiritual, the psychological, and the outer, those occurrences that will have some significance to you." He settled back into his chair and brought the tips of his fingers together. "Life," he said, "has certain cycles or rhythms much like seasons, the difference being that sometimes we spend much more time in a cycle than we do in a season. Basically we will discuss your life from the standpoints of the past—i.e., what has gone before—the present—i.e., where you are right now—and the future, which is where the cycle is leading you in the course of the next few years."

Catherine folded her hands in her lap. At last.

"If we go back five years to 1948, that marks approximately the beginning of the cycle you're in right now. 1950 brought about some changes that are still going on both internally and externally and will have to be resolved before you can complete this cycle . . ."

She tried to single out 1950; to put her mind to it. Wasn't that the year they took the trip to Yosemite? The year she and both children were held in contempt for two endless weeks because they couldn't keep up as they trudged from camp to camp, couldn't tend their gear properly, couldn't roll their sleeping bags into the required tight cylinder? Yes. The Consumate Woodsman, proud holder of the Order of the Arrow, found them soft and inept and said so each evening at the fire circle. It was, Catherine recalled with a dull ache, heartbreaking to watch Becky and Max—how old were they then? Ten? Twelve?—to watch them struggle in the Sisyphean effort to return to the warmth of his good graces. But it was she who had annoyed him most, in their tent at night reading *War and Peace* between chess moves, capturing queen after queen with a distracted nonchalance that picked at a tender place deep inside him and finally drove him, lumbering like an outraged bear, into the darkness of the forest.

Yes, she supposed there were some changes, internally and externally, the summer of 1950; certainly it was the first time she suspected that her husband disliked her.

". . . Basically," the professor was saying, "the next eight months will be a continuation of this pattern, then you'll go into a transitional period—all told, about twenty-nine months. That should end this overall period and pull you into a more solid cycle. This time is what I would call a Self Cycle, a time of reevaluation, of regrowth, of rebirth, a time of change. So, ultimately when you pass the period, somewhere twenty-eight, twenty-nine months down the line, you will have completed this growth and will emerge as almost a new person, in terms of your own inner strength, terms of how you view yourself. A self that will be much different in terms of confidence and capability." He paused and beamed approval on the grand future person she would be. "But of course in the meantime you still have to deal with today and with this period." He leaned forward. "Do you understand what I'm saying?"

Catherine stared at him blankly. "Does this mean he's not coming back for twenty-nine months?"

"Who?"

"My husband. My husband has gone off with another woman, that's what I came to see you about. Will he be gone for twenty-nine months? Is that what you see?"

The professor shook his head. "I can't tell you that, my dear. I can only tell you that whatever happens, there will be a more competent new you to deal with it."

Catherine felt betrayed. "But don't you see into the future?"

He closed his eyes. "I see certain patterns, certain highs and lows in certain cycles and experiences. I see you—past, present, and future. I see your children because you carry them with you for all time in your aura. I see your parents . . ."

Catherine snapped to attention. "My father is dead," she said bluntly, "and I've not spoken to my mother for over seventeen years."

"Nonetheless," said the professor, "you carry them with you. They are kin, you see. I cannot see the activities and the influence of someone not related to you."

"But he's my *husband*," Catherine objected.

"There are no blood ties. You share no ancestors. Basically, you have no biological past together—only the genetic pact of the future." He paused and appeared to consider his words, obviously pleased with the turn of phrase, filing it away for future use.

Catherine gripped the sides of the chair and bent forward. "But can't you make something happen?" she cried. "Can't you make something happen to *her*?"

He sighed, and appeared to summon up patience and wisdom from his great reservoirs. "That sort of thing," he said, "is not in my line."

"I don't mean anything—well, you know—permanent," she said quickly. "I just want her to . . ." She fumbled for words.

". . . to move to Pittsburgh," he supplied. His patient smile was growing slightly bored.

Catherine felt the warmth of the chair she sat in—perpetual warmth, she imagined, from the many women who had sat stiffly on the edge of it, facing this man, not giving a damn about their inner growth or transitional periods or undernourished auras. Just wanting the *answer*; just wanting to know when HE was coming home again; just wanting the good, wise professor to look into the future and see THAT WOMAN run over by a large truck next Tuesday morning.

He was thoughtful. "Yes, I know." He took a pen from a jar on the desk and wrote on a slip of paper. "As I said, that's not in my line. You can call this number, if you like."

He came briskly to his feet, crossed over to her, and bowed from the waist. He took her hand and she thought for a moment he would press it to his lips. Instead he placed the slip of paper in her palm and folded her fingers over it. "Our time is up," he said. "I strongly advise more protein. It will help pull you through the rest of this difficult cycle."

CATHERINE WAITED until Friday night. That is, she carried the slip of paper around with her, stuffed in her wallet, moved into her pocket, smoothed out and placed by the telephone, then hastily returned to the wallet when she heard the distant voices of her children. But on Friday night they went out to dinner with their father. He hadn't come in, just honked from the curb like a taxi driver or an ill-raised teenager.

For almost an hour after they drove away she prowled the empty house, rattled dishes in the sink for company, turned up the radio so she couldn't hear the familiar sounds the house made on moonless nights in early autumn.

"The next twenty-nine months will be an adjustment period," she told the cat. The cat blinked his yellow eyes as if to say that such things were already known to him. "You're not supposed to be up on the counter," she added, but without threat or even real interest. The cat yawned. That too was known to him.

She dried her hands and thrust them into the deep pockets of her skirt. There it was, folded over and handled so many times the numbers were smudged. She went directly to the telephone, took a deep breath, and dialed the number. There was an answer before the end of the second ring; a deep guttural hello. She opened her mouth to speak but her throat tightened as it always did on unrehearsed speeches.

"Hello?" the voice insisted.

"Yes," she said, as if poked from behind. "I wanted to make an appointment."

There was a pause. "Who are you calling?"

"Well. I don't know. I mean, I got this number from Professor Scarlatti."

"Yeah?"

"He just wrote down the number, he didn't give me any names. He said, well, he said it was out of his line. What I wanted was out of his line."

"Yeah? What's that?"

Catherine thought about hanging up and getting drunk instead or going off to bed and trying to sleep or crossing over the hedge and weeping the night away at Caroline's kitchen table.

"You there?"

"Yes," she sighed, longing for just a small piece of her more capable, more confident future self. "What I want," she said, "is for someone—a woman known to me—to have a really bad time."

Laughter crackled in her ear. "You wait, okay? I got to look at The Deva's appointment book. You wait."

Catherine waited, listening intently to her own shallow breathing, feeling the heat of it returned to her. Her arm began to ache as the phone and the wait grew heavier.

"Okay," the voice said, finally. "Eleven o'clock on the pier . . ."

"Not tonight?" she interrupted. "I didn't mean tonight."

"There's a bench twenty-one paces beyond Neptune's Cove . . ."

"Tonight?" she repeated.

"Tonight. Eleven o'clock. Bring a hundred dollars. No checks."

Catherine ordered her objections: Where was she to get that much cash this time of night and she couldn't meet a complete stranger on the pier in the dark. It was *dark*! And how would she recognize—who was it? The Deva? Did he say The Deva?

The voice at the other end waited until she had sputtered to a final stop. "Be on time," it said and was gone with a firm and final click.

At ten minutes before eleven, Catherine huddled on the bench twenty-one steps from Neptune's Cove. Muffled sounds of laughter and music came to her from inside the Cove when people opened or closed the door. Otherwise there was only the sound of the surf striking the pilings and pulling out to sea again. She shivered inside her husband's old trench coat, a cast-off, worn and no longer acceptable, like herself. She was cold and she was afraid; afraid of being robbed or raped or most likely murdered, her body flung onto the rocks below, her bones consigned to the deep.

But she continued to wait.

Her wallet had yielded a ten-dollar bill and some change. Caroline, clearly disgruntled, had loaned her—just until tomorrow—another ten and what she scraped from the depths of purses and pockets and drawers brought the total to $33.47. The balance had come from her children's hidden treasure: twenty-four dollars from the false bottom of Becky's jewelry box, her savings from baby-sitting; the rest from Max's coin collection, including the silver dollars that had been left him in his grandfather's will. Tomorrow, or the next day, she would confess and do whatever penance her children required of her, but tonight she had no choice.

Eleven o'clock came and went; five after; ten after. She sighed as she checked her watch in the flame of her cigarette lighter. Maybe she had been saved from being the worst kind of thief. She sorted through her conscience for signs of remorse. They were there along with gnawing regret for past and future acts of petty treachery.

But she continued to wait.

At eleven twenty-five a great bulky form moved out of the darkness. In the block of yellow light that shown from the Cove window, Catherine could make out that it was the figure of a heavy-breasted woman, covered by a long, flowing robe and wearing an Indian headdress that trailed behind her, its feathers bouncing and flapping like wings in the ocean breeze.

Catherine stared, open-mouthed. "Are you The Deva?" she whispered.

The giant woman only grunted as she sank down on the bench, then from someplace deep in the folds of her robe she pulled out a length of leather cord and a drawstring pouch.

Catherine took a deep breath and began to explain herself and her situation.

"I know," The Deva said abruptly. "You listen. I talk."

Catherine was instructed to gather nine hairs from the groin, or if that was not possible, from the head of the man in question and to carefully tie each one into the five square knots she would then make in the cord, all the while concentrating on the image of the victim. Then on the night of the first quarter-moon she was to take the cord into the garden and bury it, along with the pouch of herbs and fuchsia berries, seven inches into the soil.

Catherine interrupted to say there was some mistake, that it was not the man she wished to harm.

She was silenced with a brisk wave of the woman's hand. "You listen. I talk. On seventh day you have man come to you. Just before he come you dig up cord and untie knots."

Catherine blinked. "What's to happen?"

The Deva looked impatient and rose to her feet. "Victim will suffer impotence as long as cord is tied and buried in earth. Virility and desire return immediately in presence of woman who untie knots." She held out her hand, palm upward, and Catherine, suddenly jubilant beyond words, reached into her trench coat pocket and drew out a paper bag of money.

The Deva took the bag and stuffed it into the drapery of her skirts. As she turned to go she held up a warning forefinger and told Catherine that if the other woman's magic was uncommonly strong then Catherine would perhaps need a greater spell to overcome it.

Catherine laughed and hugged the cord and the pouch to

her breast. With the first lightness of step she had felt in weeks, she danced over the wide boards of the old pier and drove home with the chill wind blowing through the open windows onto her radiant face.

THE NEXT MORNING she squeezed fresh orange juice, made sausages and eggs for Becky and Max, then sent them off on cheerful errands. Moments after they had gone, she swept back the covers of the double bed in which she had not slept since the night he left. On his side, near the foot, she found imbedded in grainy pieces of lint, five dark silky hairs. She examined the sheets like a craftsman searching for flaws, but no more hairs were to be discovered. In one of the bathroom drawers, however, there was a brush left behind in his hasty departure, and a harvest of its bristles brought the number to the necessary nine.

She practiced the square knots on shoestrings, following the directions in the encyclopedia. Each day she practiced and by the time of the quarter-moon she was expert in fourteen different kinds of knots. Should they be needed.

On the morning of the seventh day she called him at his office. Unable to reach him—he was out with a client—she left word for him to stop by that evening right after work. It was a matter, she said, of the utmost importance. At five-thirty she went into the garden and dug up the pouch and the cord, undid the knots, and carefully placed the hairs in a white envelope for safekeeping.

Shortly afterward he rang the bell, rather than using the key she knew still dangled on his key ring. At the sound, her hands went to her hair, like those of a young girl expecting her first caller; then they smoothed the blue silk shirtwaist—the one he liked, the one that was, he had said in happier times, the exact shade of her beautiful eyes.

She opened the door, smiled, and turned, fully expecting

him to follow her, overcome and filled with passion and with gratitude for his sudden deliverance. But he stayed in the hall-way, right by the door, hat in hand, shifting his weight from one foot to the other.

"Oh come on in, silly!" she said playfully. "How 'bout a drink?"

No, he didn't want a drink. Or coffee, either. He didn't want anything, thank you. What did *she* want?

She smiled again, thinking the tardy magic would take effect any moment. Surely it would work better if she could just get him into the living room, to the crackling fire she had built in the proper way with three logs; where June Christy was singing their songs on the stereo; where the dim light of approaching dusk fell across the couch, its down pillows plumped and doused with a mixture of musk and lavender. She watched him anxiously for signs but he grew restless and irritated before her eyes, demanding to know if she'd got him there on false pretenses. She'd said "utmost importance." He'd thought it was one of the kids.

She gripped the leather cord hidden in her pocket and felt a cold chill pass through her as she remembered The Deva's words about the other woman's magic.

"It's Max," she lied. "I'm concerned about Max."

"What about him? He seems fine to me."

"He stays out late. Sometimes."

"How late?"

"Well. Midnight. Eleven."

"He's fifteen. He's growing up."

"I know that, but . . ."

"Let him have a little freedom before he gets caught up in the rat race out there."

"But on school nights . . ."

"Yes. Yes, I suppose you're right." He ran his fingers around the brim of his hat. "I guess it isn't easy for you either."

Maybe it was happening. Maybe the magic started off

94

with a kind word. But no sooner had he spoken than he put the hat on his head, tipped it back causing a shock of dark hair to escape from the front of it and fall like a boy's over his forehead.

Catherine felt faint with longing.

"'I'll talk to him," he said, and was gone before she could recover.

THE DEVA said that either Catherine had tied the knots wrong or perhaps something stronger was required; the stronger the dearer, of course. After exhausting all other possibilities, Catherine wrote to her mother and asked for the loan of two hundred dollars. It was the first real correspondence between them since Catherine had dropped out of Stanford in her junior year and eloped to Reno with an insurance salesman she had met at a Deke alum party. Afterward, when Catherine brought her groom home to Cadyville, Emily wouldn't let him in the house. The three of them stood out on the porch, and Emily— to the man's face—said her daughter had married beneath her potential. Catherine said if her mother didn't apologize she would never speak to her again. Emily said she had never had cause to apologize for anything and didn't plan to start now.

Because Catherine had been reared to act correctly in such matters, she had sent an announcement for the birth of each child, but had returned her mother's letters and gifts unopened.

Emily Gladkov responded with the money immediately, so moved by the desperate brevity of her daughter's request she did not even ask its purpose.

There were several meetings on the beach twenty-one paces from Neptune's Cove. The conclusion of each one brought back that first lightness of step and joyful ride home to Culver City. There were also several more requests for money until at length Emily Gladkov brought herself to ask if her daughter was in some kind of trouble.

. . . No, Catherine was not in trouble; it was simply a small misunderstanding.

. . . Was she sure? Travel was not easy, but Emily would come if she was needed?

. . . Her mother was not to worry. Please! And how was she? And how were things in Cadyville?

. . . Well. As for Cadyville, it was the same. As for herself, there were days when the arthritis was so severe she needed both canes to get from her bedroom to the kitchen. She hardly ever went down to the newspaper office anymore but she still wrote the obits and sent them in by the housekeeper. But no matter, she would come if Catherine needed her.

. . . No. Catherine was fine. Really, Mother, just *fine*. But she'd been wondering lately. Wondering about what her mother had said at the funeral, and about all those nasty pieces of gossip about Daddy. Was it true? True that he'd been to visit Miss Vida the night he was killed? True that he and Miss Vida were more than just friends?

. . . Perhaps Catherine could come to Cadyville for a visit? They could have a good long talk? And bring the children?

. . . Yes, of course. Yes, she would come, but not just yet.

And thus the threads of the many years of estrangement were woven into long weekly letters that passed between mother and daughter until at length they formed a whole and common cloth.

AFTER THE Great Five Hundred Dollar Spell misfired and caused instead an earthquake that rattled dishes from Long Beach to Calabassas, The Deva said that with Catherine's inclination to screw up and against such invincible strength as the other woman possessed there was only one path open to them: Catherine would have to collect the footsteps of this mighty sorceress; it was the only sure way to dilute her energy. It was clear that her feet had received such a potent blessing that the only way to overcome her power was to steal it from their soles.

For a fleeting moment Catherine questioned that it was the feet of her rival that attracted her husband. But The Deva was keen on her latest solution and Catherine was of a single mind.

The Deva's feathers rattled when Catherine reached into her trench coat pocket. "You do not pay for this spell," she said. "Loss of power if money changes hands. Leave it under bench when you go. Not for spell, this money, but for cost of precious ceremonial jewels. Here!" She held out a large flannel bag. "And here!" A sheaf of papers folded into a thick triangle was handed over. "Memorize words on paper, then burn and add ashes to bag of herbs." She placed a restraining hand on Catherine's arm and grunted, "And try to follow directions this time."

USING ONLY CUNNING, guile, and manipulation, Catherine learned from Becky the address of the woman of the enchanted feet.

"Oh Mom!" Becky cried. "I wasn't supposed to tell you. Daddy didn't want you to know Max and I had met her."

Catherine gently smoothed her daughter's hair. "Have you been there?"

"Not inside, Mom. Just in the car to pick her up." She lowered her eyes and added apologetically, "She's gone out to dinner with us a couple of times."

Catherine's own pain was no match for the look of misery in her daugher's face; the misery of being forced to betray either one or the other of the two most important people in her life. She smiled sadly as Becky, in atonement for transgressions not her own, pronounced, "She's silly! And dumb! She has a big nose."

Catherine thanked her daughter for this loyal outburst but of course she didn't believe a word of it. The woman was —of course—young, beautiful, brilliant, rich, wise, and capable of simultaneous orgasm without fudging.

SHE MEMORIZED the instructions which included intricate incantations to draw down the moon, chants to be sung over the bag of herbs, and prayers to the seven Olympic Spirits. Catherine thought it could do no harm to add some prayers of her own making.

On the first night of the full moon she anointed herself with a mixture of witch hazel, soot, and what The Deva had described as the fat from an unborn goat. Standing bony and naked before the bathroom mirror, she pulled the *bigghes*, the precious ceremonial jewels, from the flannel bag. Chanting softly, she set the narrow crown on her head, fastened the blue glass beads around her neck, hooked the bright cuff bracelet around her forearm, then drew on the leather garter with its seven buckles of silver. Then, still following the instructions, she stared unblinking at her image in the mirror until she completely disappeared.

It was eleven-thirty—nearly time. She was to gather the footsteps during the hour of Mars when that sign would be in conjunction with the Moon. It was the best time for deeds of destruction. Even though she was invisible, it would be prudent, she decided, to wear the trench coat—just in case the spell ran out, say on Wilshire Boulevard. Thus, bejeweled, begartered, and bare of foot, she drove to 24th Street in Santa Monica.

It was a small white cottage with a picket fence in front

and geraniums that needed, Catherine noted with pleasure, vigorous pruning. She drove by slowly and parked at the end of the block. Clutching her herb bag and a second leather pouch, she moved lightly along the sidewalk on the opposite side of the street, muttering the appropriate chant over and over, absorbing the power of the moonlight that slanted through the trees. There was a porch light burning four houses down from the white cottage but otherwise the whole neighborhood appeared to sleep soundly behind drawn shades. When she came even with the house she crossed the street and dropped to her hands and knees just outside the gate. There she removed her trench coat, bundled it up, and stuffed it under a bush. She peered through the pickets into the yard, snaked her arm up and over and felt for the latch, undid it, and slowly pushed open the gate, asking Aratron, the spirit who governed such things, to turn to stone any dog prone to barking that might be abroad. Not forever—just until she had finished her business.

There was a winding brick path from the gate to the porch. She took the first leather pouch and sprinkled a bit of its herb-ash mixture onto the walk. She repeated this five different times in five different places before the outline of a footprint appeared and gleamed up at her. With a brush made of sweet broom she swept the powder and the print into the second pouch. Three more footprints went into the pouch before she was done.

Then she sat back on her haunches, lifted her palms toward the heavens, and gave thanks to Phaleg who tended the affairs of Mars.

A light went on inside the house. Catherine abruptly left off chanting and dove into the geraniums. She heard the sound of a bolt being drawn, the click of a key in the lock, and then the door creak slowly open. Squinting through the leaves, she saw the shadowy figure of a woman—mortal from all appearances, and a little dumpy—step cautiously onto the dark porch.

The woman looked up and down the street, then slowly took in the front yard, at one point staring straight at Catherine's hiding place.

Catherine yelled silently at all seven Olympic Spirits. The woman shivered, rubbed her arms briskly, then shrugged and went back into the house.

Catherine waited for the light to go off inside, then stiff, her knees bruised and aching from the hard bricks, she crawled to the gate, fumbled in the bushes for her coat, and finding it threw it like a cape over her shoulders. With it flapping behind her in the mild spring wind, she flew off into the night.

SHE ALLOWED her face no expression whatsoever when Becky told her that Daddy's girlfriend was in the hospital.

"Oh really? What's wrong?"

"It's her feet. They got all blistered and infected somehow. She can't even walk on them."

"Goodness," said Catherine. "How awful for her!" And she smiled on the messenger and said, "How about prime rib tonight and baby carrots and mashed potatoes and apple pie?"

Becky flushed with pleasure at the prospect of her favorite dinner. Then she frowned and Catherine knew she was searching her mind for more bad news about Daddy's girlfriend to offer in return.

ONCE THE GREAT MAGIC had been diluted, the lesser magic was simple to perform. Poppets made from the still unwashed bed sheet, stuffed with a mixture of motherwort, rosebuds, and fuchsia berries, then bound hip to hip with a scarlet ribbon, and the leather cord, knotted and buried in the garden, between them, brought him back home, toe in sand, hat in hand, before the beginning of summer.

And they lived happily ever after.

Until . . .

Until the commonplaces of marriage returned . . .

Until Catherine grew weary of blue silk dresses and losing at chess . . .

Until she resented having to remember to knot the cord when he went out of town on business or had to stay late at the office.

Finally she questioned the worth of something that had to be so dearly bought.

And on the first full moon of a January night, she anointed her body, donned her ceremonial jewels, stowed her image in the bathroom mirror, and drove to 24th Street in Santa Monica.

Warmed in the chill air by her own inner resolve, she marched through the picket gate and sprinkled the four stolen footsteps onto the brick path. She made a deep formal bow to the Olympic Spirits and a thorn-sharp sadness pierced her heart. She waited for the pain, which was oddly pleasant, to pass.

It was twenty-nine months to the day. Maybe that Scarlatti knew a thing or two.

Becky Valentine — Activist

Born 1940, Los Angeles, California

―――――――――――――――――――――――――――――――――

"I can see it now," said Emily. "Catherine will marry some unwashed lumberjack and spawn a houseful of dirty, snotty-nosed children, and never have time to open a book." She clutched her chest and slumped against Vida's desk. "My God! My poor grandchildren—my flesh, my blood—destitute and ignorant. Oh Vida! I could just weep!"

CHAPTER SIX

It was by accident—literally—that Becky discovered the trapdoor in her mind. She was, on a balmy afternoon in Berkeley, California, recovering in the hospital from a concussion caused by an indiscriminate National Guard club to the right side of the head.

For some reason she did not comprehend, but suspected was an Establishment form of cruel and unusual punishment, she was not allowed anything stronger than aspirin for her "discomfort," as they called it. One of her housemates, Rejoyce Eveningstar, resting comfortably in the next bed in spite of three cracked ribs and red-blue contusions splashed in ugly designs over the pale white canvas of her skin, suggested that Becky use a little yoga, then some imagery to ease the pain in her insulted head.

The imagery took considerable instruction, but Rejoyce was patient and inspired. So after a full afternoon of failures Becky got the hang of it, got herself threadlike and microscopic and made her way through the difficult crossroads in the optic chiasma, then safely over the narrow and treacherous ridge of the corpus callosum that bridged the two hemispheres. Concerning this junction, Rejoyce had warned that one misstep meant a plunge into the deep crevasse of the old reptile brain. From which no one ever returned.

At this point Becky lost her bearings and missed the site of the swelling in the cortex, and instead wandered into the far reaches of an old attic, beyond memory, where she found the orderly storage of four million years.

It was in this way that Becky discovered The Power, whereupon she dropped out of UC Berkeley where she was a prominent demonstrator against the Vietnam War, and a mediocre graduate student in psychology. She went straightaway down Route 101 to Venice in southern California where she rented a twelve-by-sixteen storefront just around the corner from the strand. The space was sandwiched between that of a psychic on one side and a store that sold handmade kites and flags of India silk on the other. Across the narrow street was an artist's loft above a Japanese grocery, and next to that the Venice News and Deli. It seemed the ideal place for Becky's new life to commence.

At one end of the shop's small storeroom there were facilities, including a jerry-built shower that rained cold water onto the concrete floor and swirled it down an open drain next to the toilet. At the other end a single electrical outlet supported a small hot plate. Becky's sleeping bag would serve as her bed and, in this way, all her physical needs would be met. Just a few steps away the sand and water and western sun would supply those of a spiritual nature. The excitement was almost unbearable.

THE SIGN PAINTER did not register the anticipated, hoped-for interest when Becky told him what she wanted lettered on the board that was to hang over her door.

"My shingle," she called it. "White background. Luminous, you know? Glowing. And bright blue letters, kinda on the royal side, don't you think?" He nodded and shifted and waited for her to get to the point. Her eyes sparkled with the stars in them and her long dark braid swung out over her shoulder as she drew herself up tall.

"Lives Edited," she announced.

"Lives Edited," the young man repeated after her and wrote it down with a stubby yellow pencil in his small spiral notebook. Then he spelled it out.

"That's correct," Becky told him. And she waited for him to question her further.

"I can have it ready tomorrow," he said, and he tucked the notebook into his back pocket. "Ten bucks up front."

Becky dug into her macramé shoulder bag and handed over the money. "You might mention it to your friends," she said. "You know, if any of them have problems with living."

He smiled a little and Becky thought of James Dean. "Yeah," he said. "Sure. Well, I'll see you in the morning." He turned to leave, then turned back. "Hey," he said, "does she know?" Becky looked puzzled. "Does she know you're moving in on her territory?" He motioned with his head to the shop next door to Becky's.

"Oh, she's a fortune-teller," Becky said scornfully. "I don't do that kind of shit. I'm an editor. It's entirely different."

The young man shrugged, held his fingers up in a sign of peace, and said again that he would be back the next day. Becky watched him walk away, admiring the long, trim lankness of him, the easy set of shoulders, the golden arms that bulged out of his sleeveless white shirt. She licked her lips, then chided herself and said under her breath that she didn't do that kind of shit either. Not anymore. Hers was now a higher calling.

Inside the shop she inspected the peeling walls and saw them as their imminent shade of soothing blue. Again the excitement rose and then spilled over into her bloodstream and rushed through her body. She was astonished that no one had discovered all this before, and a little terrified by her responsibilities. She saw very clearly that the shrinks had it all wrong.

107

Since one's future was inextricably affected and directed and determined by one's past, the only way to alter that future was with editorial adjustments in that past, or for uncomplicated cases, the present. You just blue-penciled out painful things like divorces or favored siblings or glasses worn in the sixth grade. Pain was not something to be understood, to be hauled out on demand two times a week, pulled and poked at, and wooled half to death. No. No, indeed! You just hired Becky to edit your life and take all those excised paragraphs and store them up behind the trapdoor in her attic. Trashed them like boring old sins in Becky's attic, then moved free and new and unencumbered through your own house.

She sighed and felt the hard lump on her head, all that remained of the violence that had preceded her passage from wild-eyed liberal to Republican entrepreneur. "If you'd been tending to your own business, it wouldn't have happened." That's what her father would have said. At least she imagined that's what he would have said. Maybe, worse, he wouldn't have said anything, would simply have looked at her out of dark, disinterested eyes. She wasn't sure just what he would have done, what he would have said. Already he was receding and fading from under a heavy slash of blue pencil.

By early afternoon the walls were a soothing reality. Becky rented a small U-Haul trailer and drove to the Akron in Culver City to buy furniture and what she called "appointments." A woven grass rug, three giant floor pillows, a small white plastic desk, and two canvas director's chairs came to $203.46, which left exactly thirty-four dollars between her and starvation. Or at least between her and her mother's doorstep on Midvale Avenue.

After she had unloaded, arranged, admired, and rearranged her purchases, she returned the trailer, placed an ad in the Venice throwaway, then thumbtacked twenty-seven copies of her xeroxed flyer to the local bulletin boards.

Pleasantly exhausted, she bought a hot pastrami sand-

wich and a carton of milk from the Deli, then walked down
to the beach where she watched the sun slide into the water.
Becky was not in the least surprised when this produced, on
the horizon, an elusive green flash. She took it as a sign.

DURING THE next three days, only the sign painter visited Becky's
office. His name was Jimmy. But she had, well, *divined* that.
The sign was luminous, as she had requested, and the letters
royal blue. But fetching as it was, it brought no one in.

Jimmy allowed himself to accept a cup of coffee when he
brought the sign. He returned the second morning with hot
bagels and a friendly interest in how lives got edited. The third
morning, he admitted that he had some problems with living
and inquired about her fee.

"I'm just starting my practice," Becky told him. "I could
give you some kind of opening-week discount."

"How 'bout dinner at the Deli? They owe me for my
work and I take it out in trade."

With only $12.42 remaining in her shoulder bag, Becky
thought dinner would be ample payment. Jimmy sank down,
as he was directed, onto the big pillows. His problems, it
turned out, centered on a girl named Rosemary, who was small
and blond and sweetly fragile on the one hand, but on the
other, had hardened into steel with the notion of getting married to Jimmy and going back to Oklahoma City from which
place they had both fled two years before. Her father ran a
Buick agency there and had connections at General Motors.
With his help Jimmy could have his own dealership in no time
and Jimmy and Rosemary could have a big house and a big
garage with two Buicks and they could get started on a family
and the serious business of living happily ever after.

"The thing is," said Jimmy, "I don't want to sell Buicks
or live in Oklahoma City. I like my sign painting. I really like

it. There's something pure and uplifting about a well-made sign. I'm not talking about billboards, mind you, and *ad*vertising." He wrinkled his nose as if something smelled bad. "I mean good honest signs that say who you are and where you are and what you do." Becky nodded gravely as she considered this spiritual side of signs, something she had not thought of before. "And I like the life here," Jimmy went on as he unrolled a pack of Camels out of his T-shirt sleeve, took one, and offered the pack to Becky who shook her head. "I paint a few signs when I need the bread, play volleyball on the beach with my good buddies, smoke a little fine Humboldt grass from time to time." He blew out a long stream of smoke and moved his head from side to side. "No sir! I don't want to get stuck on some fucking corporate ladder when there's all this good living to be done."

He leaned forward with a proud and earnest expression on his face. "You got to understand, Becky. I'm no bullshit aspiring artist. I'm a painter of fine signs."

Becky listened carefully, mentally editing Jimmy's story as he told it, making occasional notes on her pad. She saw this as a simple, straightforward case of the Present. The obvious solution was to send Rosemary to the attic. But as Jimmy talked on that did not appear to be the problem as he saw it. He wanted to paint his signs and he also wanted to hang out with Rosemary. Yes, he wanted Rosemary all right, but without the babies and the Buicks.

Becky lifted her shoulders and shook her head. "I can't edit Rosemary's life, Jimmy. Just yours. I can't rewrite relationships. What I do is delete unwanted events and people. That in itself changes the future. Do you see?"

Jimmy didn't see, but they went out to dinner anyway. Becky watched him over the edge of her roast beef on rye, and she admired the way his slow smile began, finally breaking into a full-mouth grin, showing his big even teeth. She admired his straight nose and his noble forehead when he turned his head to the side, and the high Indian bones in his cheeks. She found herself drawn, like a hapless moth, to the hot light in his eyes.

They stayed until the Deli closed, drinking Heineken's and holding hands while Jimmy talked less and less about Rosemary.

THE NEXT MORNING when Jimmy stopped by for coffee, he found the door locked and a card scotch-taped to the window that said Becky was with a client. The hands on a plastic clock indicated she would be available at ten. Jimmy had a job in Hermosa and a volleyball game in Malibu, so he didn't return that day. The next morning he found Becky again with a client, and again the next.

Jimmy shrugged, bought some bagels, and stopped in to see Rosemary at the frame shop. It was this circumstance, a stitch dropped by the inattentive Fates, that saved Becky from her own biology.

BECKY'S FIRST CLIENT presented a difficult but exciting challenge. He was a thirty-two-year-old veteran of the Korean War who had not held a job since his honorable discharge for psychological reasons and who, every night, awoke in a darkness made cold by sweat and shattered by screams. The edit required twelve sessions in all, but at the end he slept through dry, peaceful nights, and in less than a month was working as a mechanic at the Mobil station on Washington Boulevard.

The Korean veteran was only the first of Becky's successes. Her appointment book was full and satisfying, satisfying except for the lack of payment for services rendered. Most of her clients were on unemployment or welfare, usually as a result of what needed to be edited. They would pay, of course, once they got on their feet—once there was something left over from garnisheed salaries and back child support. But meanwhile, Becky's rent was overdue and she was eating cold soup and showering by kerosene light.

Dragging reluctant feet up the stairs to her mother's garage apartment, Becky thought of how she had intended to come—in what glory and with what gifts! With French wine and a grand basket from the gourmet section at Gelson's, with a pure silk blouse to match her mother's Wedgwood eyes, and with the means to move her into a swanky apartment out on the marina.

Catherine's face filled with dismay when she heard Becky's story. "Oh, Becky, darling, I don't get paid until the first." She paced from the breakfast table to the kitchen window, back and forth as if expecting some solution to attend her. She turned quickly. "Your father? Did you ask your father?"

Becky heard her mother's question, but it made only a vague impression on her brain's machinery. There was no defined synapse, no quick jangle of recognition.

"Huh?" she said.

But her mother was pacing again. Then she stopped abruptly, picked up the teakettle, and ran it full of water from the Sparklett's bottle. "We'll have a nice cup of tea," she said quietly. "A nice cup of tea. And some toast. Wheat or sourdough, darling? Oh yes, tea and toast and apricot perserves." She smiled benignly on her daughter. "And you'll tell me about all the wonderful, exciting things you're doing."

Becky tossed her braid impatiently and her mother brought a forefinger to her lips. "We'll think of something. It will come to us. Don't rush it."

What came to them was Becky's grandmother. And that night by candlelight, Becky, as her mother had done more than a decade before, wrote Emily Gladkov asking for money.

Five hundred dollars, twice the amount requested, came immediately by wire and was followed by a note in Emily's delicate hand and reflecting her even more delicate sensibilities, wanting to know if her granddaughter was in some sort of trouble.

... No, Becky wrote back, she was not in trouble. It was just that there were more expenses involved in getting her practice started than she had anticipated ...

... Now, was she *sure?* came the question from Cadyville. Travel was not easy, but Emily would certainly come if she was needed ...?

... No, her grandmother was not to worry. Please, Nana! And how was she? And how were things in Cadyville ...?

... Well. As for Cadyville, it was the same. As for herself, the arthritis was much improved with the new medication. She did nicely with only one cane and she walked, weather permitting, down to the newspaper where she was once again writing all the obituaries and even doing an editorial from time to time as the community required or deserved it. She was quite occupied, but she would arrange to come if Becky needed her.

... No. Becky was fine. Making great strides in her career. Really, Nana, just fine ...

... And how was Becky's mother? When Catherine had been in Cadyville for Christmas—and by the way she hoped Becky would be able to fit the holidays into her busy schedule next year—she had looked tired and peaked and, if the truth be known, shabby. Was she working too hard? Confidentially now, did Becky suppose her mother needed money?

This particular letter went unanswered for several days while Becky formulated the necessary pack of lies with which to respond.

... No. Catherine was fine. She had this terrific job at the studio and a spectacular apartment overlooking the park and she had lots of nifty boyfriends for a lady in her middle years.

Becky tossed her pen onto the desk and sprawled back in the canvas chair.

"Sheee-it!" Of course Catherine looked tired and peaked and shabby. Six nights a week she led people to their tables at the restaurant. She brought them their drinks and totaled up their checks and on busy nights she bussed and stayed for cleanup. She was tired and broke and peaked and shabby. But she was also muleheaded. And she suffered from inherited pride.

That was when it came to Becky why she had been given the Power—so that she could rescue her mother—for no other reason than to make her mother happy! What Catherine needed was a real good edit!

"OH, BECKY," Catherine laughed. "I don't want to get into that sort of thing. I'm just fine, dear. My life is quiet and uneventful. That's the way I want it."

"You work all night and sleep all day. You call that living?"

"You're exaggerating. I read, I go to the theater, I take my walks." She paused. "What would you have me do?"

"Let Nana give you some money. You'll get it when she dies anyway. Why not some now? And get out of that goddamn restaurant. Oh, Mom, it just blows my mind when those tweezer-heads refer to you as The Help—like you were their property or something. Take a trip! Go on a cruise where there's some rich widowers! Fall in love! Have your hair done!"

Catherine smiled. "In that order?"

"Oh, Mom."

"Becky, I have no wish to fall in love. With a rich widower or anyone else. What's wrong with my hair?"

"It's blah. Why don't you want to fall in love?"

Catherine was thoughtful. "Well. Come to think of it,

the falling-in can be rather pleasant. Considering the loss of sanity involved. But the falling-out, my dear, is a real trial. It's like a sliver you get under your skin and you can't get it out. So there's this bump there where the body has tried to protect itself. Anyway, I think I've lost the knack to do either."

"Just let me try, huh Mom? If you don't like it, I'll put everything back like it was."

Catherine smiled again. "It sounds as if you're talking about rearranging the furniture. Would you like some soup, dear? I made it yesterday. The flavors should be nicely melded by now."

"Please, Mom. Will you just think about it?"

Catherine rose from the table and started toward the refrigerator. "Yes," she sighed. "I'll think about it."

IN THE NEXT WEEKS Becky didn't once let up. Over toast and preserves, over hearty vegetable soup, and, when Becky got her first check that didn't bounce, over prime rib with mashed potatoes and baby carrots, Becky kept at her mother with the tenacity and tender zeal of one who knows what is best for another.

At length Catherine became restless. Distracted over the Double-Crostic, she would turn on the television for the noon movie, but her mind wandered about the room and out the window where the starlings thieved in the apricot tree. A new novel from the library, the one for which she had put her name on the list and had waited with fine anticipation for six weeks, slid with an unnoticed thud to the floor.

Her life, mean and spare, was acceptable as long as there were no alternatives. Oh but the possibility of something *else*! That ruined everything. Damn it, Becky! Damn it all!

The following Sunday afternoon, Catherine settled back uneasily on the big pillows in Becky's office. In brief, clearly rehearsed sentences, she presented her father's alliance, she called it, with Vida Austin to Becky for deletion. The cold war with her mother was neatly trimmed out and smooth transitions inserted. A sexual encounter with a professor, which had produced an A in political science as a gift for Emily Gladkov and which still brought the dark stain of shame to her cheeks, was cut from her days at Stanford. Next, the theft of $66.53. There were other deletions; Becky found them innocent and trivial but she struck them from the whole. Harsh words to a cleaning woman, letters unanswered and gifts returned. And then came the big cut—almost fifty pages worth of the husband Catherine had neither forgiven nor altogether finished loving.

CATHERINE HAD her hair done, and went to the Bahamas with a nice, balding dermatologist who caused her to giggle—like a silly girl, she said—and to buy satin underthings with lace trim. Becky saw them off at Los Angeles International. She waved and grinned at the blind windowpanes of the airplane, then drove back to Venice and back to work.

Business was brisk. She repaid her grandmother and deposited a small, comforting sum in a savings account. Now, with her mother's affairs in order, so to speak, she could concentrate on a plan that had seeded in her mind when she had edited mortal combat from the life of her first client.

She composed a long letter to the Joint Chiefs in Washington in which she carefully outlined her scheme for ending the war in Vietnam—perhaps war for all time. It would require a great deal of tedious and exacting work, she explained, and she hoped they could see their way clear to furnish her with a staff of researchers and secretaries. But the design itself was clear-cut and simple; to edit from the history of the human race each and every battle—civil, border, international—to edit out each occasion in which man had declared war on his fellow man. With no history of organized conflict, with no knowledge of it, it would soon fade from the collective consciousness of the people, and the world would be at peace for all time to come.

Days went by and there was no reply from the Joint Chiefs. Becky sent off reminder letters, referring to her original correspondence and emphasizing the need for all haste. Weeks. And still no answer. Becky finally realized that if the world was to be saved, she would have to do it herself. She went every day after her last appointment to the History Library at UCLA, and there labored tirelessly, listing on yellow pads of paper all the wars she found in the books: the dates, the armies, the losses, the debts. When she had filled up three tablets and finally completed the Viking raids of the ninth century, putting the dead at seven million, she began to enter the list in her mind's attic. But that very weekend, Lyndon Johnson and the Joint Chiefs and some of the members of McNamara's Band "reached a consensus"—as the president was fond of saying— to up the troop commitment in Vietnam by fifty thousand.

Becky was exhausted from discouragement and sleepless nights when her mother came unannounced into the office. "What's wrong?" Becky cried out, leaping up from her desk and rushing to where Catherine slumped in the open doorway.

Catherine anxiously looked her daughter up and down, then echoed her words. "What's wrong?"

They enfolded each other in a careful embrace, each finding sharp bones and no substance. Then Becky led Catherine to the pillows and they sank down opposite each other, eyes wide, astonished and questioning.

"I've been working my tail off," Becky explained. "So many clients . . . and I have this project . . ."

Catherine sighed and some of the worry lines smoothed out of her face. "You're sure you're not sick?"

Becky shook her head. "No, I'm not sick, just sick and tired. Are you sick? God! You look terrible! Where's Dr. Nettlebaum?"

"I'm not sick. I know I look terrible. Dr. Nettlebaum

is . . ." She shrugged, the whereabouts of her lover clearly unimportant. She leaned toward Becky, tears standing in her eyes. "I must have them back," she sobbed. "You've got to give them back to me." Becky stared at her mother. "My *memories*," Catherine cried. "You've got my memories!"

"They're not good memories, they're just regrets."

Catherine's lower lip quivered. "I want them back."

"I don't understand, Mom? They only made you miserable."

"I want them back," Catherine repeated. "I know they're *there*, there's the outline of them in this white space where something used to be. I'm always looking for them, trying to piece things together. It makes me crazy. Oh, Becky! I am so terribly burdened without them."

Without further argument Becky returned Catherine's father, Peter Gladkov, and her teacher, Miss Vida, along with the bad years with Emily, the affair with the Stanford professor, the unkind words to the cleaning woman, the cards, the gifts. When she got to the stolen $66.53, her mother said quietly that she wouldn't be needing that, but she reached out eagerly for Becky's father when he was handed over at last. Then she raised herself off the pillows and gazed around the room like someone returned to health after a long illness. She leaned down and touched her daughter's hair, smoothing it back.

"Come for dinner," she said, smiling. "We are under-nourished."

A FEW DAYS LATER Becky wrote to the Joint Chiefs advising them of her resignation, telling them that she could not complete the job she had set out to do, that the future of the world rested once again in their hands, that it had come painfully to her attention that the memories of sadness and wrongdoing and even unspeakable horror were necessary, else both individuals and governments went on endlessly repeating their mistakes. She nodded with satisfaction as she signed her name. Then she thought for a moment, tapping her pen against her teeth, before adding a postscript. "We need our regrets."

EARLY IN AUGUST, Becky sublet the storefront to a nutritionist who dealt in macrobiotic diets. On a Friday afternoon, after she had closed her savings account and arranged to sell her furniture, she wandered along the beach saying her goodbyes to the sand, the western sun, to the delicious possibility of the green flash.

Jimmy was playing one-on-one basketball at the park and she stopped to watch him. A pretty blond girl—Rosemary, it had to be Rosemary—sat crosslegged on the grass, her eyes tracking Jimmy, as did Becky's.

He soared around the court and Becky suddenly saw him, not bare-chested above the white shorts that stretched across his narrow behind, but in a three-piece suit, with a button-down shirt and a thin striped tie. He carried a leather briefcase as he climbed the rungs of a ladder to the very top where there was a house and a garden and a dishwasher. And Rosemary, unknowing, without even a clue, removing the eagle's wings as easily as pulling them off a butterfly.

"Twenty-one!" he shouted, jumping high in the air, his arms widespread. He grinned in Becky's direction, as if to say he'd known all along she was there. She grinned back, bobbed her head at Rosemary, and moved on.

She phoned Rejoyce Eveningstar in Berkeley to ask if there was room for her to crash in the old Victorian house on Dwight Way. Yes, there was room and Becky was welcome and there was a demonstration scheduled for Tuesday. She packed her car, closed the shop, and dropped the keys off at the Deli, then drove to West Los Angeles to say goodbye to Catherine.

She let herself in and to her surprise found Dr. Nettlebaum there, stretched out watching television. He didn't get up but waved and smiled like a man who belonged on her mother's couch.

Catherine came out of the kitchen humming, carrying a beer and a mug all frosty from the freezer. She didn't notice Becky. Her eyes were trained in tenderness on Dr. Nettlebaum as she, ageless handmaiden, held out the mug to him, tipped it slightly, and let the beer slide down the side. He patted her bottom fondly, and she plumped his pillow.

Becky stood silent, and her surprise grew. How curious. How very curious. There was so much to understand about people and love. How mysterious it all was.

Catherine laughed deep in her throat at words whispered in her ear, then turned and saw Becky. "Darling! You should have let me know!" She bustled toward her, arms outstretched. "But that's all right, you can share my steak and I'll put in another potato."

Dr. Nettlebaum swung up from the couch, shoving his feet into his flip-flops. "Absolutely *not*," he said. "We're trying to get some weight on you. I'll run over to Trader Joe's and get another one."

"No," Becky said quickly. "I'm not staying. I'm off to Berkeley, just wanted to kiss the mother goodbye."

"You didn't tell me," Catherine objected, guiding her daughter toward the kitchen. Dr. Nettlebaum grunted, picked up his beer, and turned back to the news.

Becky shrugged. "Well, it was kinda sudden."

"But your business. I thought it was going so well?"

Becky shrugged again. "I've given that up." Her mother looked at her sharply. "I've returned the memories to everyone who wanted them. Except the soldier. I've given him my address in case he needs his."

Catherine said, "Are you going to open an office in Berkeley?"

"No." Becky shifted her weight and looked at the ceiling.

"I'm going back to school," she said finally, "back to what I was doing, you know. But—" She paused and tried to order the words, tried to think of how to describe the loss.

"What is it?"

"Well. I've decided to work within the system."

Catherine nodded knowingly. "How hard that must be. You've such a gift."

Becky shook her head. Her eyes were a hundred years old. "I am too ignorant for the gift," she said. "I have no wisdom." She gazed down at her feet as if into a grave. "I am," she said, "a danger."

LATE THAT NIGHT Becky stopped in San Jose for coffee to prop up her eyelids and take her on into Berkeley. She sat in a high booth at the back of the empty restaurant, and there, once again, made the journey through the optic chiasma and over the ridge of the corpus callosum, on up beyond memory to the old attic. She retrieved her father from the bin where she had stored him and then she closed the door and locked it behind her.

DORIAN BLAKE—LIBRARIAN

Born 1929, Santa Barbara, California

Simon Cole brought with him to the desert his three children, Regina, Claudia, and the youngest, Dorian—his favorite—who was the sweet golden image of her dead mother.

CHAPTER SEVEN

In the beginning Dorian tried having her father at home, tried sincerely and earnestly for two wretched months. She turned the den into a comfortable retreat which Simon Cole had accepted with distracted, sad-eyed gratitude and about which her family had set up a wounding howl.

"But I don't like the television in our bedroom," her husband said. "Watching in bed gives me a stiff neck."

Dorian reflected on Stephen's stiff neck which seemed to her to be of a congenital, not to mention terminal, nature and unaffected by television one way or another.

"And just where am I supposed to entertain my friends?" said her daughter, a senior in high school whose friends arrived each afternoon in troops and gaggles to drink and feed. When Dorian suggested the living room as a likely place to gather, Brenda had scowled that it was so out in the open, that there was no privacy whatsoever.

"The old loony wanders in and out like a lost soul. It's mortifying, Mother. Totally mortifying!"

"Then use your own room," Dorian snapped, in a rare show of anger.

"It's minuscule, Mother. Totally minuscule."

"He's always turning things down," her firstborn, Paul,

complained. "He creeps around the house turning things *down*. The stereo, the air conditioner, the lights . . . And he closes the drapes, Mom. We're living in a tomb."

Dorian explained, in the quiet, unruffled voice she found useful in family politics, that her father—their *grand*father, she reminded them—was unaccustomed to so much activity, that light and noise bothered him. And—be fair now—that he was no trouble, not really, that most of the time he stayed in the den with his books, fixing his own meals and having them there on a tray, keeping from underfoot as he put it, asking nothing of them but to be driven once a week to the public library.

Thus Dorian managed to keep up her end of the argument with the children. But her husband, having announced that he felt unwelcome in his own home, finally and simply made his point by straying. He was obvious and outrageous about it, coming in late two, even three nights a week smelling of a good time.

SHORTLY BEFORE her father had come to stay with them—a circumstance brought about by the sudden death of his second wife, and "a temporary thing just until we can make other arrangements"—Dorian Blake, with the good form she required of herself, marched upon her fortieth birthday, and during the passage had, with matter-of-fact calm, assessed herself as uncommonly ordinary. On the bleak heels of this observation she began to wake in the dark hours of early morning and pad about the house on bare, numb feet, sipping warm milk from a mug. Wondering if anything would ever happen to her.

She wished she was the sort to have an affair, to thrash about in wild abandon in the long afternoons of silk sheets and mirrored ceilings; she wished she could rise into a cleansing frenzy over what her husband was doing, and wished she cared a fig about who he was doing it with; she wished she had a passionate desire to take up serious painting, but it seemed to her that her life lacked colors to splash in its honor across a canvas. And one morning just before dawn on what she called her milk runs, she realized that what she really wished for was to get into her car and drive and drive and not look back; drive until she came to a place where a stream would rush to her, where the wind would say her name as it passed, where— where, oh dear God!—where something would happen.

When she heard this wish spoken aloud from her own lips, she felt the hard thud of panic in her chest. She feared not so much for her sanity—although she questioned that too—as for her fine sense of the rightness of things. That very day she made an appointment with her internist who examined her, ran a battery of tests, and when the results confirmed the perfect health he suspected, patted her hand and spoke cheerfully of early menopause. He gave her a prescription for Valium and told her not to worry.

She tore up the prescription, willed herself to sleep through the nights, gave up smoking, and took up rigorous exercise. She applied for and got a part-time job in the research library at the university. Dorian Blake, a tall, fair woman with even features and clear blue eyes, a handsome woman who dressed and behaved like the dowdy matron she believed herself to be, felt it must come as no surprise to anyone to learn that she worked as a librarian.

"WHY CAN'T your sisters take him?" Stephen demanded.

Well. Well, the truth of the matter was that Regina and Claudia had even less filial feeling for their father than Dorian, and none of her crippling sense of obligation. When Dorian had approached them with the idea of sharing their father's care, Regina, a biologist at a remote station in Surinam, researching monogamy in New World primates, and Claudia, recently divorced from her third husband and looking for a fourth on guided tours, both begged off, citing time, space, and—Regina at least, who had a wide streak of honesty—inclination.

Because Simon Cole had long been diagnosed as a schizoid personality, subject to episodes of borderline withdrawal, he granted his daughter Dorian the power of attorney that had formerly rested with her stepmother. And with this power and to keep peace in her family and for his own good, Dorian—accusing and convicting herself every step of the way—found a place for him and convinced him that he wanted to go there.

On Sundays she made feeble attempts to draw Simon into conversation. He would slide down in the chair by his bed and listen to her attentively out of his eyes, two cool spots of intelligence in his expressionless face. He would nod politely, answer yes or usually no to carefully phrased questions about the food and the care, then appear to be genuinely saddened when she rose to leave. She took cookies which he nibbled obediently and books which he accepted reverently, greeting each one as an old friend. No, he did not want a portable television; no, he did not want a radio. Just the books. Thank you, Dorian, just the books.

So she brought them. The cookies and the books. She would pause in the doorway as she was leaving and watch him sort slowly through the new stack. Looking frail and breakable in the slanted light. Dorian ached.

ONE SUNDAY she encountered the director in the hospital parking lot. He was middle-aged, ruddy, and athletic; jovial, she thought, for a psychiatrist and not, she had noted gratefully on the day her father was admitted, overly given to jargon. As they chatted pleasantly in the afternoon sun, he told her, to her doubting amazement, how good her visits were for the patient.

"No, really," he insisted. "For a couple of days after you

come, he eats well, he's friendly, cooperative . . . He's down-right spritely. Really, Mrs. Blake."

"I had no idea," said Dorian. "I assumed it was just as painful for him as it is for me."

The doctor shook his head, ignoring, or too cagey to acknowledge, her mild complaint about her own problems in the matter. "No, your visits are good for him," he repeated firmly. "Maybe you could come more often? Do you think you could make it twice a week?"

"BUT WHY can't Paul do it," Brenda whined in a put-upon tone she had lately perfected. "Why am I always the one to be burdened with the domestic chores?"

Dorian sighed. "Paul has volleyball practice on Wednesday afternoon. You know that, Bren."

"Then you could see Grampa on Thursday."

"You have your piano lesson on Thursday."

"Exactly, Mother. I'm talking about priorities. I'm going to *be* a musician. Paul is not going to *be* a volleyball player."

"I'm trying to space the visits," Dorian said wearily. "Sunday, then Wednesday. The middle of the week."

"Thursday is just as middle as Wednesday, depending on which end you're coming from." And while her mother puzzled on this piece of reasoning, counting on her fingers backward and forward from Sunday, Brenda flashed on an idea. "Why don't we just have pizza. You could pick it up on your way home."

"Your father doesn't like take-out for dinner. He says it makes the family seem fractured."

"So let *him* cook."

"Oh, Brenda—"

"Really, Mother, women have come out of the kitchen, you know. Families are sharing household responsibilities. They are no longer assigned by sex."

Dorian set the iron on its heel and smoothed the white eyelet cuff of her daughter's blouse. "Oh?" she said. "Tell me about it."

IN AN EXPANSIVE GESTURE, Paul agreed—for only a small increase in his allowance—to take care of Thursday night dinner. But only if the meau was left entirely in his hands. As it turned out, Paul's idea of a casserole was to open cans of something by Franco American, sprinkle Parmesan cheese on the top, and bake for twenty minutes. After three such Thursdays, Stephen began to have dinner meetings with colleagues and Brenda would find herself invited to a friend's house. Dorian and her son would eat together at the breakfast bar in the kitchen, where they began, at this late date, to enjoy each other's company.

SHE COULDN'T SEE that it made any difference, these twice-weekly visits. Simon was as uncommunicative on Thursdays as he was on the weekend. But then one Sunday, she found him on the small walled-in patio outside his room. Her glance took in the lunch tray on the table beside him and she felt the quick maternal satisfaction that comes of a clean plate before she noticed that he held his head in his hand in a gesture of despair.

"What is it, Father?" He raised his eyes to her and motioned for her to sit down. "Father?" she insisted. "Are you all right? Should I call the nurse?"

"Emma died last night," he said in a grieving voice. "Did you know?"

One of the patients, Dorian thought. She nodded sympathetically and patted her father's hand. "No, I didn't know. I'm so sorry."

"Such a terrible death. There was nothing I could do for

her. Justin saw it happen, saw her take down the blue jar and swallow the arsenic. But the fool didn't tell anyone! That clumsy idiot! That stupid donkey! I was too late. Poor Charles. And their child, the poor child!"

Dorian continued to pat his hand and to utter soft disconnected sounds as she grew more and more bewildered. Arsenic? Oh dear! You'd think for the price they charged there'd be better security.

And then she saw the book lying open, face down on the table, the title leaping out at her like a living thing. She felt a chill pass through her and she took in her breath and held it.

"Poor Emma—poor, poor Emma." Simon rocked as he mourned. "Little more than a child herself. A tragedy. Such a tragedy."

Dorian let out her breath slowly, keeping a watchful eye on the book. "In the classical sense, Father? Is that what you mean?"

"If only Charles had called me sooner. If only that bumbler Canivet had not administered an emetic!"

"You must not blame yourself," Dorian said carefully. "Emma was doomed. Growing up on that isolated farm, a sentimental girl full of romantic notions about how her prince would come for her. She could easily have mistaken Charles for a prince, his old nag for a white horse."

Simon's head came up with a jerk and there was a cunning expression about his eyes. He reached for the book, took it tenderly in his hands, closed it, and held it out to her. "What's done is done," he said quietly. "You'll see to the arrangements, won't you?"

DORIAN THOUGHT about it and decided not to tell the doctor. She had searched for weeks before she found this small hospital that served the mildly deranged, the neurotics who didn't fit into Sunny Acres or Peaceful Pines yet did not require the locked wards and the shock treatment of the more hopeless facilities. The staff might not look kindly on delusions about suicide—even literary ones. So when she saw the director in the hall the following Thursday and he asked how the visits were going, she smiled and replied that her father was coming along splendidly. Just splendidly!

That Thursday Simon was courtly and charming as he ushered his daughter onto the patio and rang for the nurse as for a servant, requesting tea. In no time at all, Dorian realized that she sat across from the most famous of all foundlings, Tom Jones. And she listened with outright pleasure to his misadventures along the road to London.

Later that evening at the breakfast bar over what Paul called Mexicali Delight, Dorian told her son what had happened.

"Gee, I don't know, Mom, is this a good idea? I mean what if Grampa thinks he's Ahab and you look like a big white whale?"

Dorian laughed. "Oh Paul, he isn't dangerous."

"I don't know. Maybe you ought to talk to the doctor about it."

Dorian shook her head. "They'd probably fill him full of Thorazine or something. Don't you see, Paul? He's *alive*! He's *talking*! Okay, it's fiction, but at least he's talking. Why, I haven't heard so many words out of Father since we lived in the desert."

"Was he—? You know. The Wizard of Oz or somebody then?"

Dorian laughed again and held up her fork. "What did you do to this? It's delicious!"

Paul grinned. "You really like it? A girl in my chem class told me about it. You just mash up some Hormel tamales and put in a can of drained corn and some green chilies and salsa, then throw a couple of eggs at it, grate a lot of Jack cheese on top, and cook at 350 'til it bubbles."

Dorian leaned back and rubbed her stomach. "No, he

wasn't the Wizard of Oz. I don't remember him all that well. I was only nine when we went to the desert. After my mother died, Father left the university and took a job at the Indian school."

"On a reservation? I didn't know that! Hey, Mom, how come I didn't know that?"

Dorian's smile was fond and indulgent. "Well, you must admit you haven't shown much interest in my past—boring old ancient history that it is."

"I'm interested now. Did you go to school with the Indians?"

Dorian nodded. "And Father tutored us. Father and the other teacher at the school. Miss Vida. Miss Vida Austin—a giant of a woman with great coils of red hair. Of all the teachers I've had she's the one who stands out in my memory. Monday was my favorite day of the week, because it was time to go back to school. Can you imagine?"

Paul shook his head emphatically. "Not in my wildest dreams."

"We thought we were going to have her for our very own. One night, not too long before we left the desert, Father told us that he and Miss Vida wanted to be married. He asked if that was all right with us—if we would like to have Vida for our mother. We were so pleased—so happy—so excited." She shrugged. "But nothing came of it."

"How long were you there?"

Dorian looked up at him out of thought-clouded eyes. "Four years," she said slowly. "A little over four years."

"That's really cool. Living on a reservation! How come you left?"

"Your grandfather had a nervous breakdown and had to go to the hospital. Regina went off to college, and Claudia and I went to live with Aunt Claire in Santa Barbara. We didn't see much of him after that. I really know very little about him." She looked up with a wan smile. "Sad, isn't it? My own father and I don't know anything about him." She was silent and thoughtful as she tried to call up the Simon Cole of the past, the young professor, thin and wiry, with his fat mind and rich tongue. She sighed. "But I do know that he was happy then." She rose to clear the table and Paul reached over to take her plate.

"I'll get the dishes," he said. "You look tired."

"Why thank you, Paul. That's very thoughtful."

"Listen, Mom, I'm sorry for bugging you about Grampa. If you want to bring him home again, it's okay with me."

Dorian looked at her son, all long bones and disputed hair. She wished for spontaneous gestures; small loving acts. She wished she could hug him, wished there wasn't that white expanse of Formica between them that would make it awkward and studied. She shook her head. "We'll see," she said. "Meanwhile we'll try to get your dad and sister to Thursday night dinner." She winked at him. "They just don't know what they're missing."

Paul carried the dishes to the sink and spoke with his back to her. "I kinda like it this way, Mom."

Dorian was quiet. So did she—oh yes—so did she! There was something disloyal going on here. A small, unseemly rip in the family fabric. She stiffened up her spine and stepped back.

THE NEXT SUNDAY Simon presented himself as Dmitri Karamazov, raging against that old buffoon, his father, Feodor. "He has robbed me of my inheritance and now he sniffs after Grushenka, a woman less than half his age!"

Dorian eased into the part of the gentle Alyosha, the peacemaker who forgave everyone—a role not unlike a mother's and one well known to Dorian. But when they reached the trial she found that Simon's grasp of the politics involved far exceeded her own, so she sat quietly and listened until she was roused by the rattle of trays in the hall and the chill of early darkness.

"Oh dear," she said. "It's late, Dmitri; that's your dinner coming."

She started to rise and Simon reached out and took her arm. "My father said I would grow up to be a garbage collector. He said I would never amount to anything."

"Dmitri?"

He smiled. "No. Simon here. *Who has not wished for his father's death*. That's Dmitri." He closed his eyes and leaned back into the shadows. "Would you bring me some Dickens next time, please Dorian. And some Henry James I think. A little of the Russians goes a very long way."

DORIAN CHANGED her mind; she made an appointment with the doctor. Her concern, she told him, was that this sort of thing might lead to a breakdown. She had no idea what had precipitated his illness years before in Arizona; she only remembered that he was in high spirits before it happened. And he could, by stretching the imagination, be considered in high spirits now.

The doctor didn't think there was any danger of Simon becoming psychotic. Of course, schizoids did slip into schizophrenia, but her father had good neurotic defenses. Dorian looked at him blankly. "What I mean," he said, "is that a neurosis in many cases will prevent a psychosis." He pointed to a stack of files on his desk. "I don't know what happened in Arizona either. Not exactly, but according to the history it didn't produce a full-blown psychosis. He was never completely out of touch."

"But now? You know. Madame Bovary and Dmitri and . . . Do you call that being in touch?"

"I call it a schizoid mind at play. Many of them have a

wonderfully rich fantasy life. Your father is an extremely literate man, wondrously well read. It seems natural to me that he would people his very spare life with all these characters he knows so well. He's safe with them, they offer no surprises, they are no threat to his self-esteem. He can open up the book and let them out, then herd them back in and close it behind them when he's had enough." The doctor leaned back in his chair, obviously pleased with his assessment of the situation.

Dorian was unconvinced. "But shouldn't he be talking to you," she said. "I don't know what to say to him. I don't know the proper responses. What if he would say something that would unravel the mystery? You know, of that breakdown in the desert? A sudden insight?"

The doctor chuckled and told Dorian that she had seen too many bad movies, and that as a matter of fact, these episodes were confined to her visits and were probably for her benefit, that probably—yes, very probably—Simon was trying to learn to talk to his daughter.

"Look," he said, "I'm not saying that this is the most satisfactory way for a man to spend the last years of his life. But it's not a bad compromise."

"Then you don't think he'll get well?"

"I think he is well *enough*. Mrs. Blake, it is often a mistake to demand more health of an individual than that individual is capable of achieving."

DORIAN GAVE UP her job at the research library so she would have more time to read the novels her father requested. She had no wish to be caught short again, with her ignorance hanging out like a shirttail, as it had with the *Brothers Karamazov*. She increased her visits to three times a week, then to four, and almost without noticing it, slipped into a daily routine of breakfast with the family, reading until lunchtime, long afternoons with Simon, dinner prepared by Paul, then more reading in bed until she fell asleep. For the first time in years, Dorian was content.

Not so Stephen:

"Why don't you just move in out there at the funny farm?"

To which Dorian replied smoothly, "You know, Stephen, I mistook you for someone else. I thought you were a prince and I thought your Pontiac convertible was a white horse."

And not so Brenda:

"Other mothers are *home* when their children come in from school. Or else they do something vital like being a psychologist or an architect or something." In this manner, Brenda covered both the traditional and the liberated. And found her mother speechless at both stands.

Paul changed his major from prelaw to home economics. He stopped smoking pot, saved his money, and started a collection of cookbooks, beginning with the Larousse *Encyclopedia.* Paul was ecstatic.

Not so Brenda:

"Other mothers make balanced meals, Mother. I've gained ten pounds since Paul started doing the cooking. Mother!"

And not so Stephen:

Stephen placed chefs just one tiny notch above hairdressers. They were okay but you wouldn't want your daughter to marry one.

"Oh come on, Stephen," said Dorian, looking up reluctantly from *Heart of Darkness.* "That's such a cliché."

Stephen nodded as he loosened his tie. "Isn't it just. But what do you expect? A cliché is what I've become. And you. And us."

And thereafter the Blakes went their separate ways, taking little notice of one another, speaking in short, polite sentences from behind their separate sections of the morning paper. Sometimes, Dorian would muse upon it all in an idle, distracted way. She would consider her children from under hooded, thoughtful eyes, reflecting on the flesh-and-bone signs of a joyous merger of genes, and she would question the passing of the passion that had produced the unit, the affection that had sustained it.

Dorian wished for the grace to wish her husband well.

SHORTLY AFTER CHRISTMAS, Simon began to undergo a change, one for which the doctor said Dorian could take full and honorable credit. He began reading the *Christian Science Monitor* and the *Wall Street Journal*. He checked with his broker daily and treated Dorian to a detailed commentary on the market. He ordered a twenty-four-inch television installed in his room and hurled invectives at the screen as he and his daughter watched Richard M. Nixon inaugurated as the thirty-seventh president of the United States. He was happily consumed with the weather, with politics, with each and every world crisis.

Finally, after he had clicked off the television and analyzed the news for Dorian's benefit and edification—she drumming her fingers on the bleached oak of the chair arms and trying to stay awake—he interrogated her about Stephen and the children: a barrage of questions that did not wait for answers. He had been himself for almost two months when Dorian admitted that she was bored with him; admitted that she found him cranky and garrulous and forgetful and self-centered. He's *not* getting better, she told the doctor, he's getting just like everybody else!

To Dorian's growing annoyance, which she took small pains to disguise, Simon asked often after her sisters.

"Ah, my sisters!" said Dorian one Sunday afternoon. "Well, dear Regan is still in the jungle in South America, and Goneril is off on a Princess Cruise to Yucatán."

Simon looked puzzled.

"*Regan* and *Goneril,* Father," she said impatiently. "Don't tell me you've forgotten them?"

Simon scratched his head, then his eyes lit up. "Oh yes, yes of course—*King Lear!* Well, well, my dear—"

Suddenly inspired, Dorian rose and sunk into a deep graceful bow before him. *"How does my royal lord?"*

Simon held up his hands as if to fend her off. "No, no, oh no, Dorian. I don't want to do that anymore."

"How fares your majesty?" she insisted.

"Now Dorian, why don't you turn on the news there and let's see if the Concorde got off the ground. Maiden flight at Toulouse today."

Dorian shook her head. *"How fares your majesty?"* she repeated.

Simon hugged himself tightly in the long, empty silence. Then he covered his face with his hands and spoke through the hatching of his fingers. *"You do me wrong to take me out o' the grave,"* he said softly. *"Thou art a soul in bliss; but I am bound upon a wheel of fire."*

Dorian leaned over and gently pulled at his hands. Her eyes were bright as with a fever. "Your majesty, it is I, Cordelia. *My love's more richer than my tongue."*

He sighed and jerked out of her grasp. "You would have us mad, would you not? With your voices ever gentle, soft and low. I cannot do it, Dorian, I cannot. I have to live in this world. Poor as it is, I must live in it."

Dorian went to her knees before him. "Father, listen!" She placed her palms together as if in prayer. *"O, look upon me, sir, and hold your hands in benediction o'er me—"*

Simon stared at her fearfully, then rose and took awkward, desperate steps toward the door. *"We two alone will sing like birds i' the cage,"* he cried. "Is that what you want, Dorian? Is that the speech you're after? Talk of prayer and songs and old tales? Talk of gilded butterflies?" He turned to face her directly, his hands held in fists behind his back, his legs spread wide to hold his ground. "I will not, Dorian. *That way madness lies*—no more of that!" He paused. His face crumbled and sunk in upon its cheeks. "Forgive me. I must save myself." He closed his eyes and leaned against the wall. *"Here I disclaim all my paternal care . . . And as a stranger to my heart and me Hold thee for ever."*

DORIAN LEFT the hospital and did not return; she took to her bed with her books. Paul delivered the cookies along with requested volumes of the Durants' *Civilization* and Churchill's *History of the English-Speaking Peoples*. Paul and his grandfather played Scrabble and Monopoly and watched the Smothers Brothers and became good friends.

In the spring, the director wrote a letter saying he could no longer justify accepting a fee for the care of a man in such sound condition, both mentally and physically, as Simon Cole. In June, Simon and Paul went to Paris where Paul enrolled in the Cordon Bleu and Simon read in the sunshine of their small garden on the rue de l'Université. Brenda was accepted at Juilliard and Stephen fell into some kind of obligatory love with his twenty-two-year-old secretary.

Dorian, who had caused these blessings, rose up from her bed, got into her car, and drove; looking for a place where a stream would rush to her and the wind would say her name as it passed.

REGINA COLE – BIOLOGIST

Born 1924, Santa Barbara, California

Jane Eyre *was not obliged to whet the intellectual appetites of the Cole girls. Rather, Vida found herself happily scrambling to keep ahead of them, especially the eldest, Regina, who drank up Vida's lessons like a saguaro in a spring rain.*

CHAPTER EIGHT

THE ANIMAL INCHED ITS RIGHT FRONT FOOT FORWARD APPROXI-
mately twelve centimeters and hooked it, ever so carefully, over
the branch. At seventeen hundred hours, precisely fourteen
minutes and thirty-one seconds later, it moved the left front
foot in the same stopped-down, fluid motion. There was no
more activity for the next hour; it simply hung there, like an
algae-stained tropical fruit, fastened securely to the tree by two
sets of huge curved claws.

Regina was as silent and immobile as this sloth she observed from her low perch in the tree opposite. Only her
thoughts changed position, striding about briskly to gather up
and summarize what had gone before, then leaning back to
float and wait, to let the sounds and smells drift in as she
wrapped old knowledge around them. At one point she made
the barest suggestion of a nod toward the sloth when a rare
anthropomorphic notion crossed her mind, and she saw the
two of them as old statues in a forest cathedral—ancients, arti-
facts, survivors from another time.

At 18:14:02, the animal eased its head through one
hundred and eighty degrees (this action required almost a full
minute), grinned foolishly, and looked Regina straight in the
eye. Probably not. They were, according to the scanty litera-

ture, quite shortsighted. Did it see her? Smelled her, more likely. All the same, Regina's gaze, trained to avoid the threat of direct contact, fixed on a point below the sloth's shoulder, then came down to her pad where she put a check in the column "Interaction with Observer." And because she was not only thorough, but honest, she added a question mark.

Director of this research station in one corner of Surinam's vast jungle, Regina was doing this particular duty because she was the only one of her small staff who had the discipline for it, who could tolerate the numbing boredom of it. For the past twenty-eight nights she had watched this animal from early dusk to late dawn and for her trouble had collected thirty-five lines of data. The movements of the limbs, generally in connection with browsing, took up thirty of those lines; that of bowels and bladder, four; and now this, this steadfast, cretin stare.

Regina had come late and unwillingly to sloths. Monkeys were her speciality; for more than two decades she had watched them, mostly as a part of a study of monogamy in primates; gibbons, titis, douroucoulis, tamarins, and marmosets—it was a meager list, indicating that bonding was adaptive for only a few species. It was, as her students liked to say, for the birds.

And then came the directive from the university: a lot of interest in low body temperature as a correlate of slowness in mammals—grants available from the NIH and even the space program—she was to capture a small sample, four or five subjects would be sufficient—rectal temps, metabolism, blood samples, the usual. And then some simple sequential behavioral studies in the wild state. Her graduate students could do that. Just a preliminary project—six months would do nicely.

Humph.

The sloth still watched her and though it was not good form she met its eyes. It did not blink or look away as primates tended to do, but rather seemed to grin more broadly. It was, of course, the configuration of the small rounded face that gave the appearance of good cheer: the black clown nose, the mask-like slashes across the small eyes, the jack-o'-lantern stripe that outlined the mouth and turned it up at the corners.

It was an easy job, if tiresome, its subject good-natured and benign, but producing in Regina a hollow sorrow, as when one watches a slow-witted child.

This was *Bradypus* A-3. Regina indentified her animals in this simple way, with the generic name followed by letters and/or digits depending on the size and scope of the study. She was forthrightly contemptuous of the growing number of scientists who humanized their subjects with given names, and when students commented on her outdated system and how "other people" did it, she would whisk from her girlhood in the Arizona desert Vida Austin's admonition: *If you name a thing, you mean to keep it.*

Her subjects came, not to stay, but to pass. She had never yielded to the temptation to raise a foundling, to record its progress as orphan child or hers as surrogate mother. So while the Goodalls and the Burutés and the Fosseys became the darlings of the media with their Flo and Fifi and Lolita and Ralph and Effie and Uncle Bert—Uncle Bert?!!—Dr. Regina Cole's exquisite thousand-page manuscript on *Saguinus* 0-1 through 0-480 languished on editors' desks as it made the rounds of the publishing houses.

One enterprising fellow said they might be interested if Dr. Cole could draw comparisons between monogamy in her marmosets and that in man, including an explanation for the radical decline of it in the latter. Regina wrote back that to discover the truth of rats, one studied rats; that she, for one, did not take great conjectural leaps across species—let alone *family*—boundries to speculate about "the meaning of it all."

And that was the end of that.

Dusk with its fine mist gathered like a shroud around her. She shivered, not from cold but from this promise of rain, and pulled a slicker from her pack, then a flashlight. She could

145

hear the students; their laughter floated down from the platform a quarter-mile up the path and reaching forty-five meters into the darkening sky.

They had come, this season's clutch of embryonic biologists, with their chessboards and their guitars and their pot and their dreams of glory—treating Regina like some kind of housemother. For five years she had not published and so, for them, had perished.

They had failed at sloth watching, one by one, leaving it with shamefaced apology to Regina. She watched at night, slept and struggled to keep up with her own work by day. Leaderless, without direction, the students regressed into a trio of Huck Finns and built themselves a tree house from which —they said—they would study seed dispersal and pollination. Not an ordinary tree house but a six-by-six platform that perched high in the open pavilion where the giant emergent trees pushed out of the canopy into the endless fields of blue sky. Higher than a twelve-story building, the platform was reached by a rope apparatus so ingenious as to attract the attention of *Newsweek* magazine.

The journalist had come and Regina had welcomed him, had spoken to him of her marmosets, of the sloth project. But he had looked past her, his eyes lusting after the rope.

Another Huckleberry in her Eden.

They were off of it now and coming down the path. Huck A veered off and came to stand under the spot where Regina was wedged in the tree. Slight and wiry, he was the youngest of the three but with the finest mind—agile and prehensile—and the small man's punishing need to excel.

"Dr. Cole, I presume." He bowed with a mock flourish, tossing one wing of his imaginary cape over his shoulder, brushing the ground with a plumed hat. "Hey now!" he said. "Maybe you'd like us to build you a platform up there. You'd be more comfortable, wouldn't have to hang on like that."

He was, of course, the father of that damn rope! She

relaxed her grip on the branch above her and slid it along the bark until it rested in her lap. She had selected *Bradypus* A-3 because of the animal's preference for this tree at the edge of the clearing where the sun reached the ground and allowed for low branches. For twenty-eight days the sloth had not moved from the tree or more than seven meters up its trunk; a double blessing for a biologist who suffered, of late, from a creeping rain forest arthritis and as a result, a judicious fear of heights. She suspected her students knew of her weakness and it made her cross with them.

"I'm quite comfortable, thank you," she replied, and as she felt him watching her, lifted her chin to display what had been called a formidable *grande dame* profile. It was her only physical attribute that could be so regarded. She was small and delicately boned with fair skin that unlike the bones had benefited from the moisture of the tropics, and dark blond hair caught up in a rubber band. People who did not know her, men especially, were often prompted to ask if they could help her. Could they move that, lift this, get that down, change this, fix that. Or build this.

"Just let me know if you change your mind. Well, I guess I'll be off." He started down the path, then stopped and came back to the spot beneath the tree. "Dr. Cole?"

"Yes?"

"Has she done anything?"

"Oh my yes," Regina answered. "She runs the whole gamet of sloth behavior. She is a most splendid subject." After a pause she thought long enough to be significant, she added, "You could have learned a great deal from her."

"Really?" Of the three, only he had given up with misgivings, had returned three times to the project, then thrown it over in seething frustration. "What, for instance?"

Regina craned her neck slowly in sloth fashion and looked down on him. "Patience," she said, "one of the necessary virtues of a scientist."

"Patience," he answered smoothly, "is the virtue of an ass, that trots beneath its burden, and is quiet."

Regina laughed, threw back her head and laughed from her belly. "I guess you were ready for that one," she said. "I guess you've been instructed in the virtues of patience before." He nodded warily that he had. "Well," she went on, the laughter changing from warm to cool, "I hope you're not so busy cataloguing snappy answers that you neglect your survey of the pavilion community. I am required after all to report on your progress."

"I didn't mean to be insulting."

Regina pursed her lips thoughtfully. "No," she said, "no, I don't think you did. I think you have in your head whole herds of restless ideas and from time to time they just gallop right out your mouth without so much as a by-your-leave." She paused and considered him. Her favorite Huck, far and away, no question of that. "Now, tell me, do you have any more aphorisms about patience on the tip of your eloquent tongue?"

He raised his shoulders and stuffed his hands in his pants pockets, looking like a child who expected a harsh reprimand and was at a loss when it was not forthcoming.

"Well?" Regina insisted.

"Well," he answered. "There's the one from *Twelfth Night*."

"Oh? I'd like very much to hear it."

He moved his feet wide apart and clasped his hands behind him in the stance and attitude of one preparing to recite. He cleared his throat. "She sat like patience on a monument," he said. "Smiling at grief." And before Regina could gather her wits to respond, he was off down the path.

AN HOUR AFTER DAWN had made itself known on the forest floor, *Bradypus* A-3 curled its head down over its chest and abdomen and tucked it between its legs, a signal that it was time for both the observed and the observer to retire. Regina stretched, then groaned as her joints cracked smartly. Carefully, she put her arms through the straps of her backpack, then inched her way down the ladder. She hunched her shoulders forward and rolled her neck in a slow circle. Her bones would not survive five more months of this punishment; the vampire night lapped the blood from them. Before the sloth there was only discomfort. Now there was pain.

As she neared the station the renewing smell of coffee came to meet her, followed by that of bacon frying in the heavy cast-iron skillet. Her labored steps quickened, past the showers, the generators, the holding cages, and on up the stairway. She paused on the second landing and looked out at the signs of morning spread before her, at all the breathtaking reasons for why she was still here. From this very spot she could count and name twenty-seven different species of trees; in the square mile surrounding the station she had identified over three thousand kinds of plants.

This was the forest primeval, as splendid and diverse as before the first ice age when all the earth was mantled in this eternal green. Diverse but strangely constant, with evolution slouching along at a leisurely pace, with time enough to achieve perfection, and without the push and shove of changing seasons where life had to struggle to keep up, to seek new and better ways to protect its seeds. This forest was not required to learn as many tricks as one in a temperate climate, did not have to dash into bloom at the first sign of rain or into hiding at the first chill wind. For the rain like the warmth was a given.

The constancy comforted Regina, the diversity kept her mind ever astonished, but it was the solitude that fastened her to the forest. The solitude. Even during the nine long months when the students were here, she had only to take one of a hundred unmarked paths to find it.

It was in the desert Regina had learned to love solitary places. She was fourteen years old when she moved with her father and sisters from Santa Barbara to Arizona and had turned, almost overnight, into a nut-brown athlete whose mind and body could run ten miles just from the joyous urge of it. Her father had taken a teaching job on the reservation after her mother had died under the wheels of a speeding van and Simon Cole found he could not live with the sight and sound and smell of iron murderers in the streets. In time he had put away his sorrow and, like his daughters, had bloomed on the poor soil set aside for the Apaches, nomadic warriors he was directed to turn into useful, productive American citizens.

It was the other teacher at the school, Vida Austin, who was responsible for the flowering of the Coles, which in Simon's case lasted four years. Then Vida was simply gone one bright summer morning, leaving no trace except Simon's broken mind, his shattered heart.

Shortly after, Claudia and Dorian went to live with their father's sister. Regina entered the university, and Simon was committed to a hospital for the mentally ill in Camarillo, California.

Regina finished her BS in biology at the University of Arizona, then went home to Santa Barbara for her Master's. There she fell in love and lost interest in animal physiology except where it concerned the warm flood of hormones that coddled her brain and caused her thighs and breasts to so sweetly ache.

One evening he had not come by when he said he would. Again. And when she had seen him dead of a hundred different hideous accidents, he called—after, not before the fact—to say he'd had to rerun an experiment at the lab.

But she had called the lab!

She knew he couldn't take time to answer the phone!

But it was her *birthday*, she cried out to him.

But it was his *work*, he answered. You understand, Gina. You understand.

She understood that for two long years he had given what part of himself he could spare and had expected the whole of her. She understood the folly of trying to write a thesis in this crazy state of grace. And she understood from her own experience that it never lasted anyway. People failed each other for a variety of reasons, did that or changed, or changed their minds and went away. Or through no fault of their own, they died. It was an abandonment just the same. Only work abided; it was the only single-hearted companion.

She made her choice, and mourned it with brilliant accomplishments. In connection with her doctorate she studied gibbons in Borneo, intrigued with the tender ways in which they shared parenting in what appeared to be a long-term bond. When promiscuity was the rule in mammalian nature, where was the advantage of this curious constancy?

She went on to study the phenomenon in douroucoulis in Paraguay and Argentina, titi monkeys in Brazil, then here to Surinam where she had produced her unsung study of marmosets.

By the time Regina had arrived in Surinam, her head was the absolute sovereign of her heart. There had been brief affairs with visiting scientists, satisfying, she told herself, because of that very brevity, because the scientists, like her subjects, came to pass.

As did the years.

Now there was this arthritis that would cripple her as surely as there would be three to seven meters of rain this year.

But she would stay on.

This mansion in the green half-light was her home and here was her work. Here she would stay until she died, a gnarled old fossil, and here would be buried to become forever a part of it, entombed in the great silent grave of the forest floor where she would enrich the soil and feed giants.

Regina would have denied it with her last breath if someone had accused her of harboring such thoughts. They smacked of romanticism, full of angst and hubris, and she did not dwell on them.

HUCK D, the journalist, greeted her in the common room, his face flushed with the delicious seduction of danger. She nodded good morning and made her way to the coffeepot that perked away on the stove at the far end of the room. In puppy fashion, he hurried after her.

"Coffee?" she asked pleasantly, holding up the pot, its blue enamel darkened with soot and neglect.

"I've had plenty, thank you, Dr. Cole. I've been watching for you since sunup." She poured her coffee and waited for enlightenment. In the week he had been here, he had paid her only the attention due an innkeeper. "I'm hoping you can help me," he went on. "The guys are not familiar with all the stuff up there and it would add to the authenticity of the article if I could get the names right." He smiled appealingly. "They say you know everything."

Regina stirred her coffee and nodded agreeably. "Yes, it certainly would," she said, ignoring the clumsy compliment. "Yes, by all means." She motioned for him to follow her to the untidy bookshelves that lined one corner of the room. "A local field guide should take care of that. We have a good one here, compiled over several years."

He grunted and held out his hands, the palms up, revealing angry red lines of the rope and the new calluses on his writer's virgin flesh. "We've tried that, Dr. Cole," he said. "Jesus, Dr. Cole, it's a botanical garden up there, it's a zoo!"

"So take photographs of what you want and I'll ID them."

"Oh sure, I'll just run down and have them developed at the corner Photomat. Dr. Cole, if you could just—"

"—come up on that platform with you?" she finished for him, looking offended and incredulous.

"Yes, ma'am, that's what I hoped."

"I'm sorry," she said quickly, dismissing any possibility of such a rash and foolish act. "I am truly sorry, but I simply haven't the time to go crawling around on that platform. I'm behind in my work as it is."

"But you see, Dr. Cole, I thought maybe we could include some of your work. You know, you could look at some sloths while you're up there."

"They don't go that high. They've no business up there. Nor, young man, have I."

"But your little monkeys do," he said slyly. "Your marmosets. I've seen them." Regina eyed him warily and he went on, gesturing enthusiastically. "Why, I could do a couple of paragraphs on your study. And some pictures. You and the marmosets? Whatever you say."

"How many paragraphs?"

"Well, you know, several."

"Is this a bribe?"

"Yes, ma'am."

"Did my students put you up to this?" He shook his head vigorously, his eyes round and innocent as he solemnly crossed his heart with his forefinger.

"Well," she said, stirring her coffee into a whirlpool, "I suppose I'll have to give it some thought."

DUSK FOUND Regina climbing the ladder to her usual perch, but *Bradypus* A-3 had moved to a higher branch, and—for a sloth at any rate—seemed agitated and restless, emiting little birdlike cries—*eee, a-eee*—at regular intervals.

Damn! She took a deep breath, then rotated her ankles, flexed her knees, and massaged her right elbow. Sometimes for no reason it locked into place, useless for climbing, for reaching, for hanging on. Cautiously she pulled herself up, using her left arm to bear most of her weight, pushing with her feet. Puffing from the off-balance effort, she eased one leg over a branch, straddled it, and hoped that it was sound. She adjusted her pack and looked down at the ground. There, smiling up at her, was Huck A.

"She up there?" he called.

"Yes, she moved higher."

"Okay if I join you? Will I chase her away?"

Regina snorted. "That's rather doubtful," she said crisply. "In one rare instance where a mother rushed to her threatened offspring, she was clocked at an amazing four meters a minute. Yes, of course, come on up."

With effortless simian grace he scampered up the ladder, then shimmied onto a branch opposite Regina. Smiling, he reached into his shirt pocket and pulled out a candy bar. "CARE package from home," he explained cheerfully, handing it over. One of his large front teeth slightly overlapped the other and this, combined with a determined cowlick and perpetually arched eyebrows and the green leaves that framed his face, caused Regina to think of elves.

"It's very kind of you to share it," she said as she opened the dark outer wrapping, unfolded the white waxed paper, and with obvious pleasure broke off two squares. She nodded her thanks and handed the rest of it back to him.

"Okay if I watch for a while?"

"Welcome to," Regina replied, graciously inclining her head as if asking him in to tea. A soft touch, that's what they thought she was, a simpleton, to be lured and wooed to her destruction with Hershey bars and the promise of public notice in some damn magazine.

"Why do you suppose she moved after all this time?"

"That's what I hope to determine. Perhaps there was an impetus or perhaps she just moved."

He nodded, slid off the wrapper, opened the inner one, and broke the bar, handing her half. "They don't really care about that, you know," he said, looking very wise. "Natural history is dead, just like God. High-tech physiology is where it is today. We need to understand how mammalian tissues adapt to low metabolic rates." He looked up and motioned with his thumb. "That's what that sloth is good for. You need to be on veeeeerry low energy output for space travel."

"Do tell?" said Regina, using direct eye contact.

He blinked and looked away. "I'm not saying that's what I think," he explained. "Or how I think it should be. I'm just telling you how it *is*. You've been off down here for so long you don't know about the changes in the world. Oh, I'm not saying that you're not highly regarded, Dr. Cole. But your stuff is too subjective for the journals and not jazzy enough for the popular press."

Regina lifted her chin and displayed her profile. "Well, I am gratified that I am at least still a subject of conversation— tatty old hat that I am."

"That's why I think you ought to go up there with Hal."

"Hal?"

"You know, the journalist."

"Oh yes. Yes, of course. Now why should I go up there with Hal?"

"Well, just imagine!" He lifted his hands and spread them as if across a marquee. "Just imagine this frail, middle-aged lady"—Regina cringed and rubbed her elbow—"climbing forty-five meters to the very top of the South American jungle to study her beloved marmosets."

"Yuck," said Regina.

"Well. Not quite that bad but you get the idea."

"Would it help matters if I were black? Had two heads? Ninety-four years old next November?"

He laughed. "Yes it would. But at least you're a woman, and blond, and good-looking. Those are pluses."

"This must be your PR hat you're wearing. You certainly do sow your seeds in a lot of different fields."

"I just figure that when I get older I may want to rotate my crops."

Regina laughed with the pleasure she found in him, so cocky, so full of himself. "All right, Mr. Renaissance Man. Why? Why have you taken such an interest in my faltering career?"

He left off smiling abruptly. "Because you started me on mine, Dr. Cole. I read a paper of yours when I was in the eighth grade and I was blown away by it. It was so correct, so precise, but it had so much . . ." He scratched his head for the word, then snapped his fingers. "Passion!" he cried. "That's it! Passion!"

Regina stared at him without speaking, reflecting on the days of her passionate papers. Who would think that the loss of love could make good science.

There was a slight rustle from above. Regina looked up quickly and there saw the reason for *Bradypus* A-3's restlessness. She was about to be joined by an untagged stranger.

Huck opened his mouth but Regina silenced him with her finger across her lips. She took the stopwatch that hung from her neck on a leather cord into her palm and pushed the button. She got the tape recorder from her pack, handed it to Huck, and motioned for him to turn it on, then she positioned her camera and began clicking away.

Bradypus A-7, as he was immediately christened, moved toward A-3 with loud sniffing. Slowly, A-3 loosened her grip on the branch and allowed her legs to ease down and dangle in space, supporting herself only by her long arms. A-7 approached deliberately, using all four limbs until he reached A-3, then he turned slowly and suspended himself in front of her.

Just moments later, Regina clicked off the watch, made a note, pushed the reset button, and clicked it on again. The courtship had ended; mating had commenced.

For the next twenty-three minutes the sloths engaged in a dour, silent copulation, grinning their separate ways into the forest. Regina recorded seven general muscle spasms in the male, though she could not be certain that meant there were seven ejaculations.

A-7 disengaged, brought his legs up, hooked them into place, then made his upside-down way along the branch. A-3 resumed her former position and began to munch on the leaves around her.

"Doesn't look like they had much fun," Huck whispered to Regina. "I mean, considering that they stayed at it for so long."

"They're not in it for the fun," Regina whispered back. "The intromittent organ of the male is quite short and therefore the sperm is not deposited deep in the vagina. A long or repeated copulation would be advantageous—"

The strained look on his face stopped her lecture in midsentence. "Oh come on now, there's no reason to look so dismayed. The function of a sexual encounter is to produce offspring. I think you better see if you can locate your missing scientist hat."

But he was looking past her, his eyes intent on the slowly disappearing sloth. "There he goes. Look at him. Not even so much as a thank-you-ma'am."

Regina felt real impatience. People, even biology students, or maybe especially, were hopelessly inclined to confuse the behavior of other animals with their own.

"He's served his purpose," she said curtly. "In roughly two hundred and sixty days he will have replaced himself— well, half of himself in the case of sloths. He has fulfilled—get out your philosophy hat—his destiny."

Huck let out a long heavy sigh and shook his head sadly. "There are some things about life I wish I hadn't learned. In a scientific way, I mean. Like this. I'd rather not know this—I'd rather not have to accept that we're all here just as the temporary guardians of somebody else's genes."

There was no arrogance now, and in its place a woebegoneness that gave Regina an urge to reach out to him. With great effort she did, letting her hand come to rest on his shoulder. From the depths of a womb that had never carried life came the undeniable stirrings of the need to mother, to protect, to comfort with hot cereal and apples, to lead onto a safe path, to welcome home before dark.

Guardians yes, but not—oh no—not mere vessels.

THE NEXT MORNING Hal was waiting for Regina by the coffeepot in the common room.

"Very well," she said, before he could again present his case. "I have some work to do and some sleep to get. I'll go up with you this afternoon." His grateful smile faded as she went on. "I want at least a thousand words on the marmosets, and I want to approve those words before you leave."

"It isn't usually done that way."

"I daresay. But that's the way we'll do it or we'll not do it at all. And another thing, your article must not in any way imply that this is a unique situation. Platforms in the rain forest go at least as far back as Hingston in 1932, and Perry's ropes in Costa Rica are far superior to what we have here. Ours are primitive by comparison. I insist that proper background credit be given."

Regina watched, not without sympathy, while Hal struggled to control his anger with her. "Dr. Cole," he said evenly, "it is my intention to be accurate."

"I'm pleased to hear that," Regina answered brightly. "Then you'll have no objection to my checking the full manuscript." She flashed him a smile of dismissal and poured her coffee.

REGINA OVERSLEPT, a rare event, and arrived at the base of the tree later than she'd intended. She called out her apology to

Hal whom she found pacing and muttering as she approached. He made a move to take her pack but she shook her head. He shrugged and quickly showed her how to get into the harness, then demonstrated the use of the foot sling and the rope ascenders.

"It's really very simple, just a pull, stand, reach operation. You see?"

She followed the length of the rope with her eyes to the barely discernible dot that was the platform. Fear crouched like a toad in her chest, ready to hop in all directions.

"I'll go first and you can watch how I do it. They keep the extra gear up top. I'll send your stuff down on the auxiliary rope." Regina nodded. "You see how to hook on here?" She licked her lips with a dry tongue and nodded again.

She forgot to time him, but it seemed only precious seconds before he called to her from above and lowered the equipment. She fastened herself into the harness, hooked on, and with a deep breath she imagined to be among her last, started the climb.

The first ten meters went swiftly and she felt the exhilaration of relief as she congratulated her cooperative bones and muscles. Soon after she detected the onset of a cramp in her left calf and stopped to rub it out. At twenty-five meters both legs were on fire and little grey specks like tiny ashes floated in front of her eyes.

She didn't have to do this! There was nothing in her contract with the university or with herself that required her to do this.

Pull—stand—reach.

At thirty-five meters she stopped again to rest. The ground, that good, dear, sweet earth, was miles and miles below her.

Pull—stand— The blinding white light of pain struck her elbow and knocked her arm from the rope.

She had not allowed herself the luxury of questioning her decision to make the climb; she knew well enough that she could come up with a rational answer. Now, by the same token she would not question her decision to abandon it.

"Hal?" she called. "I have a nasty cramp here. What do I do to go backwards?"

"Sorry, Dr. Cole, you need the descenders to go down. They're up here."

It was the first time Regina had heard a cheerful note in the young man's voice. Very well. So be it. The only way down was up.

Pull—stand—reach—

"Now this part's a bit tricky," Hal said, still outrageously cheerful, as she made the last pull-stand-reach and found herself opposite but not close enough to the platform to step onto it. "What you do," he went on, "is to make a big push off the tree and swing yourself across."

"I'm sorry?" Her voice was as small and thin as a child's. "Say that again?"

"You just push off, swing over, and catch on to this pole. Then I'll help you unhitch. But wait! First let me get some shots of you where you are. Oboy! Hey, that's ter*rif*ic! Now, let's have a big smile."

Smile? Regina was drowning in thin air. She had to be —her life was passing before her. She repeated the words to herself over and over—*push off, swing over, catch on*—as she stared into the lens and smiled weakly for the camera.

"Okay, that's great! You have this nice ethereal expression. Really great! Now, swing on over."

Regina pushed off as hard as she could and swung up onto the platform. She caught the pole with her left arm and hugged it to her, her cheek pressed against the rough surface of its face, her legs wound around it in a lover's grip. She felt the pack being lifted from her shoulders and heard the snap of the harness being unhooked. Still holding on to the pole, she slid down into a heap at its base.

There were moments in the next two hours when Regina

rejoiced in the strange beauty of the pavilion, but for the most part she thought only of the ground. A part of her brain, where discipline granted immunity to the terror that encompassed the rest of it, numbered and identified flora and fauna in the order it was photographed. One of the moments of forgetfulness came when a harpy eagle, a sudden whirr of black and silver against the sky, flew in above them to capture a careless capuchin monkey.

"Nature," murmured Hal in a reverent voice. "We're seeing raw nature in action. The saga of prey and predator."

"Rubbish!" snapped Regina, sounding like her old terrestrial self. "We are seeing nature disturbed. The monkey is providing dinner because of its curiosity about us."

Their uneasy collaboration continued but no marmosets appeared. "It's getting late," Hal said. "You want to come back tomorrow and see if we can get a shot of you with them in the background?"

She clutched the pole tighter. "I think we can do without the family portrait."

"Whatever you say, Dr. Cole. I have some terrific shots of them already." His good humor was inexhaustible as he bounced around the platform. "Okay," he said. "You go first. It's just like before except you use the descenders. You control your rate of descent, see? It's a blast!"

He talked on and on but Regina did not hear him. She was paralyzed from head to toe. More than she had ever wanted anything, she wanted off this platform, but she could not so much as move her little finger to make it possible.

She felt her face crack into a smile and her voice came to her from far away. "As long as I'm up here I may as well make a few more notes. I'll just watch how you do it and I'll be along shortly." She sounded fit and sane, or so it seemed to her, like someone tending to a few tiresome details. Oh yes you go on along and I'll join you as soon as I finish here and freshen up a bit.

She could not move.

Hal repeated the instructions, demonstrated them, then swung out on the rope with a jaunty wave of his hand and a heart-stopping Tarzan yodel, leaving Regina alone, at the very top of her beloved forest, in the embrace of her cherished solitude.

AN HOUR PASSED and was gathered into the fading light. Regina had made no move toward the rope. She was listening intently to the forest when a voice came from below.

"Dr. Cole? You still up there?"

"Yes," Regina croaked in answer. "Yes, I'm here."

"Okay if I come up?"

"Yes, please do." *Oh please do!*

It was more than fourteen minutes before he appeared on the platform. Regina knew because she had counted the seconds.

"Hal said he left you up here because you wanted to do some work." He frowned and shook his head. "It's not a good idea to be going up and down this thing after dark." She turned her face up to him, dead white in the shadows. "How come you didn't come down?" he asked.

"I was afraid," she answered.

"Well damn it, why didn't you call for help?"

Regina sighed. "Because it is not my nature." She sighed again. "This is, you see, a new fear for me. A new fear needs getting used to. My body, which has been my friend all my life, has failed me and we have not yet come to terms about it. I trusted it to get me up here and back down but my right arm has forfeited the event and my left leg has struck in some sort of support of the union they both belong to. I'm sorry if I babble. I was becoming quite lonely for the sight of a human face. One well regarded. It makes you babble."

"That's all right," he said, and ducked his head in a mixture of pleasure and embarrassment.

"I would appreciate it very much if you would help me. I'm overdue for my appointment with A-3."

He picked up her pack and put his arms through its straps. "You probably won't approve of it," he said, "but I call her Susan." He helped her on with the harness, pulled the rope over as far as it would come, and attached the descenders. "Can you support yourself on one leg, Dr. Cole? You'll have to use the foot sling."

"Yes, I can do that. Thank you. Can I operate the descender with one hand?"

"Yes ma'am, you'll get a feel for it right away."

Regina let her body go through its physical litany of rotations and flections and sorrow over past agility. Just before she swung off she considered a small prayer, but quickly decided against it. Prayers for deliverance required a long relationship of give-and-take. She had given no thanks; she would ask no favors.

She fixed her eyes on Huck, a good sight if it was to be her last one, and swung out. It felt all right. She had not plunged headlong toward the ground or dangled helplessly like a trapped parachutist. The cramp was easing up, and her arm was a good little soldier.

Yes, it felt fine. Quite fine. "I'll not wait for you," she told Huck. "I'll go straight away and see about A-3." She released the descender, trying it out, letting herself slip slowly down. Then she stopped, relishing the control.

"Susan?" she said. "Susan, huh? Well, why not?"

Huck was leaning over, peering down at her, his hands on his knees, the crooked teeth gleaming in the last light.

"Sounds to me like you mean to keep her."

Regina let herself slip again, faster this time, a short breathless flight, then she stopped abruptly. She gave a small, playful pump of the foot sling, and the rope swayed. She looked up at the place where she would never come again but would carry with her always.

"Yes," she said. "I mean to keep her. I mean to keep you all."

Megan Austin — Poet

Born 1949, Dallas, Texas

Vida was gone and I needed the memory of her as I never had before. I needed the example of her strength and independence and passion for life to get me through an impasse, a time of desolate confusion and hard choices.

CHAPTER NINE

RICKY ISSUED THE ULTIMATUM. It was the third time that week and he was getting good at it. He leaned over the breakfast bar and shouted at me that it was either him or those goddamn boxes, and if those boxes were still here when he came home that night then I'd have seen the last of him. And he didn't mean maybe.

The teakettle whistled and drowned him out. "Would you like some coffee?" I said this is my quiet, soothing voice, the one with a distant warmth. "Maybe you need some coffee."

"You are crazy," he said, putting spaces between the words and hitting each one hard. His head moved back and forth and his just-showered hair fell in lovely dark strands on his forehead. His eyes were bright green and dangerous.

He was standing in his stocking feet; he wore a Brooks Brothers beige striped shirt with the cuffs not yet buttoned; no pants; tie dangling around his neck waiting to be tended. He looked vulnerable as only a half-dressed man can. He made his voice very low and patient. "You have to choose, Megan. You have to choose."

I ground the beans, longer than necessary, poured the water over them, and set the pot on the warmer. I got two mugs from the cabinet, arranged them carefully with spoons and napkins, then turned to the refrigerator. I bustled in a cheerful, domestic way. It was too early for choices.

Or perhaps it was too late.

Ricky and I have lived together for almost five years in what we formerly called—in a smug, superior way—a sensible arrangement. My mother calls it "disgraceful" and whenever she comes out here from Dallas she stays in Santa Monica with my Aunt Effie. I am invited there for Sunday brunches and it is made quite clear that I am to come alone. I get all gussied up and go show myself to her, living proof that I may have fallen on disgrace, but not on hard times.

We are declared enemies, Mother and I. One of my earliest cogent memories is one in which she and Aunt Effie are sitting in the dark green lawn chairs under the big willow by the side of our house in Dallas. I was playing nearby—just within earshot—with that stolid preoccupation I perfected early on that caused adults to think I was off in my own world and paying their conversation no mind. They were drinking lemonade. I can still see them in their tennis whites, the afternoon breeze moving the willow-leaf shadows across their faces. I can hear the ice cubes clinking in the tall glasses as Mother confides to Aunt Effie that come-to-think-of-it, her "female trouble" came on right after Mary Megan was born. She lowered her voice and said that a woman with her narrow hips could not endure a long labor without ill effects.

This statement must have made as much of an impression on her as it did on me, for thereafter whenever I—as she said—crossed her, she would observe in a cold even voice that I had always been an obstinate child, even in the womb, that it had taken seven days of hard labor to get me born. For years I accepted this as the reason for our enmity—that she could not look at me without remembering the pain of bearing me, just as every time I looked at the rope swing that hung from the large oak in back I heard the sickening crack of my shoulder hitting the ground.

I was eighteen before I understood the real reason. Although our house had three stories and sat on over a half acre of ground, there wasn't room in it for more than one Daddy's Girl, and both mother and daughter aspired to the job.

Mother was Born Again after Daddy died of a coronary on the eighth hole at the country club. That was four years ago. She says my brother and I brought Daddy to his untimely end with worry over us, what with Chet not keeping a job and me living in mortal sin. Chet gets jobs, even good ones; he's a master mechanic and he's sold some lyrics to a rock group that plays in North Hollywood. But sometimes he just doesn't show up for work because he's gone off to hear The Grateful Dead in Red Rocks or Grass Valley. My brother is a forty-year-old Dead Head. Mother understands the expression to be a literal one. She says he is a lost soul, her cross to bear.

Gainful employment is certainly not my problem. I'm a stringer for United Press and I'm a published poet. I'm well paid at UP—it supports my poetry habit. That's another cross for Mother. The Dallas *Morning News* ran a little story about me last year, with a goosey-eyed picture and a couple of my poems. One of the poems used the words "orgasmic joy," the other, "running breasts." Mother said she was mortified to the bone and could not face her friends at bridge, let alone church, and had to come out here to Aunt Effie's until the scandal died down. Mother has had a hand in this contest that's going on between me and Ricky in that her letters abound with news of my various cousins' marital and maternal accomplishments.

In which regard: I began to notice in myself very odd behavior right after I celebrated my thirty-first birthday. That was in May and when they started running the June ads for wedding gowns and fine linens and silver in the LA *Times*, I would sit long over my coffee, lusting after Waterford crystal and Limoges and seed-pearl tiaras. I started hanging around the cribs and highchairs and strollers that contained the offspring of my friends. I could feel the slack-jawed grins on my

face as I oohed and aahed and jabbered in a somewhat de-
mented way.

Ricky and I made a pact when we moved in together five
years ago: no wedding rings, no swimming pools with big
mortgages. No babies. We made no vows to love, honor, and
cherish but rather to be forever—however long that turned out
to be—honest and open. We would be not only solvent but
sane.

We have separate bank accounts from which we con-
tribute with fastidious equality to our support. We also share
equally in all the tedious, mind-numbing chores that cause
chronic depression in middle-class American wives. Ricky likes
to cook, and to gallop through the apartment herding the
vacuum cleaner, *Aida*, his cleaning music, turned up full blast.
He grumbles about the windows and the toilets. So do I.
We've been giving some thought to having someone in once a
week so we won't have to misspend our energies in this way. I
am reminded that my mother has had someone in every day
of her adult life. It would come as an amazement to her that
we even have to discuss it.

So. We have this lovely old apartment in Westwood Village but there is nothing in it that owns us, including each
other. We are liberated.

Ricky is a lawyer, a divorce lawyer, and he hates his work
with a dark passion I've not seen him lavish on anything else.
What he really wants is to be a photographer. We've turned
the den into a studio and darkroom for him; he takes classes
and goes on field trips. His grand plan is to save enough money
so he can live off investments in second trust deeds while he
gets to be known as an artist with the camera. He pays alimony
to one wife and child support to another. It will be awhile before he can give up the Law.

Ricky is thirty-nine. He laughs and says I won't have to
worry about his midlife crisis, that he plans to go to Philadel-
phia instead. I don't quite get the connection but it strikes me

funny. He's talking about a vasectomy; we do not laugh about that. He is so unfair and wily as to use the woman's argument that it's his body and he has the legal and moral right to do whatever he wants with it. Lately, he does not trust me in this respect.

The last time Mother was out here—that was last June around the time of the Waterford-Limoges Awakening—she got to talking about Aunt Vida, how it was Aunt Vida's fault that I wrote words like "orgasmic joy" and "running breasts."

"Mary Megan, I couldn't even under*stand* that poetry. Running breasts! Why, whoever heard of such a thing. And it didn't even rhyme!"

She went on to say that she would never forgive herself for letting me spend all those summers on Grampa's ranch in Tucson, and be exposed to all those nasty books Aunt Vida had lying around.

I got to thinking about Aunt Vida and how she had lived a long, productive, and satisfying life without the benefit of husband or children. I got down the wooden box—the one she had left to me—from the top shelf in my closet and I began to fill it up with the secrets she had told me the summer before she died. It seemed to me I could find some sort of answer that way, could set my mind, if not my willful body, at ease about the baby problem.

Then I started to wonder about Vida's friend Emily Gladkov, and what had *really* happened that caused Vida to leave Cadyville. So I put Emily in the box too but she would have none of it. After all those years she still hadn't forgiven Vida for sleeping with Peter. That all happened in the days before Sisterhood, when a husband was looked upon as a prized possession, a someone about whom one could feel jealousy and rage. So, I got Emily a box of her own, and I put my mind to Malcolm McGuire's daughter Virginia, and Vida's sister Elizabeth, and before I quite knew what hit me, there were all these boxes all over the place.

Even though Ricky doesn't have a mystical bone in his body, he thinks there is something unnatural and alarming about the boxes. And I haven't found any answers. Not yet.

"IT'S YOUR TURN," I said, "but I'd be happy to fix breakfast if you're running late."

He said he didn't want breakfast, he'd lost his appetite. He wanted to discuss this.

I put my hands on my hips and said I didn't believe for one minute it was the boxes he was ticked about, that I thought it was my natural, normal, healthy, eternal, God-given drive to have a child of my own that was making him feel squirrely and guilty. Rightfully so.

"Not guilty," he said, in his sonorous courtroom voice, and brought his open palm down with a smart whack on the breakfast bar. "A college education costs fifty thousand dollars today and will probably be prohibitive in the year 2000."

"I have every intention of assuming the responsibility for my child's education."

"And so do I, madame; I am not a *breeder*." He was clouding up to rain hard. I could feel it in my bones. "Megan," he said, "I am almost forty years old. It is not just the financial investment I'm talking about. There is the one having to do with *time*. I don't want to be involved with Little League when I'm fifty. Now, could we just get back to those boxes . . ."

I COMPROMISED. That is to say, I lied. I hid the boxes at the back of the closet where my old caftans hang down to the floor, and when he came home I showed him my new orange, looseleaf notebook with its dividers and neat plastic tabs. I announced that this was where I would keep my work, and in manila file folders, and on the backs of gas bills and shopping lists like a proper writer.

It was a wrong move. When we were making the steamiest kind of love, that of reconciliation and unkeepable promises, I heard outraged voices coming from the closet. Ricky did not notice them, but they were for me a real distraction. So much for honest-and-open.

RICKY WAS PLANNING a field trip to Baja, California over Easter vacation to take stark black-and-white photographs of sea lions and shore birds and especially gray whales. His son, Richard III, was going along. Richard lives nearby in Century City with his mother, who is a lawyer, and her husband, yet another lawyer. The three attorneys, Ricky, Carol, and Gordon, all work for the same firm. We see them socially; go out for Japanese food and to the Mark Taper and the Hollywood Bowl; they come over here for Ricky's homemade pasta and we go over there for Gordon's Mongolian Hot Pot. My mother said it was the most appalling situation she ever heard of in her whole life—that all the divorced couples she knows back in Dallas have the decency to despise each other.

Ricky and Richard were involved in elaborate preparations for the trip, so Richard was around a lot. He was doing yeoman research on whales and is the kind of bright, verbal kid who likes—like his father—to have discussions.

"Megan, I have something I would like to discuss with you." Or, "Megan, could we have a short discussion before dinner?"

And he is full of questions and observations:

"Why would anybody ever think that a whale has sperm in its head?"

"How do you make miles from knots?"

"How come the female is bigger than the male?"

"Megan. MEGAN! Did you know that ambergris is found in a whale's *rectum*? And people put it in *perfume*? Aaaargh!"

So I read the books he brought from the library to prepare myself for our discussions. Aunt Vida used to say you have to keep ahead of the fast ones and behind the slow ones. I did a lot of reading.

Ricky and Richard made long lists and went shopping at Big 5; they used the word "gear" a lot, and "grub." They would stroke their chins and swagger and wink at each other. And *whisper*. They were two eleven-year-olds running away from home.

The evening before they were to leave, they packed up the rented VW van and went over their lists. We would set the clock for five A.M. because Ricky said all adventures of this nature must begin before dawn.

WE HAD A PARTY to see the stalwarts off. Carol and Gordon and the grandmothers and Chet with his new girl came for beer and pizza. Chet gets older but his girls are younger every year. This one said her mother came barefoot and pregnant to the Summer of Love, and that her water broke at a Dead concert. I figured that made her eighteen at most.

We had a fine time. Ricky showed slides of his new photographs; glorious shots of wildflowers in the high desert, and some tasteful black-and-whites of the resident nude. Nobody recognized me because I was shot through thick gauze and with foil reflectors. There was not a stitch of character on my whole body.

Even so, one of the grandmothers needed to justify exposing Richard to female nakedness. "Now, that's ART," she said, poking him on the shoulder. "*That*, Richard, is real ART!"

It was, of course, not art; it was an experiment that

failed. But then, *my* mother would have sailed out of the room, towing the poor innocent child in her wake. As a matter of fact, Richard's only comment on the nudes was that they were fuzzy.

Chet played some old Stones songs on his guitar and we all sang along, hummed mostly. I read my latest poem, inspired by one of the grandmothers' recent facelift. Everybody liked the lines "ten feet is the dissolution factor" and "she picked up a return ticket/to nineteen-sixty-five."

Then it was Richard's turn; his eyes glittered like stolen jewels and he told us of whales. He said their ancestors lived on the land and that they have gone back to the sea; that they communicate with high-frequency clicks called echolocation and that they are the smartest of all animals.

I, the teacher, puffed up with pride.

"The blue whale," he said, "is almost extinct. They live in small family groups like people used to do—the bull, the cow, and the calf."

"Maybe that's why they're going extinct," said Chet's girl.

Richard looked at her solemnly and told horror stories of unrelenting slaughter.

Carol grew pale and brought the subject back to sociobiology. "I have read that the large extended family is the highest form of social organization in nature . . . that the nuclear family is the primitive condition."

We all nodded and looked at one another in silent congratulation. We were indeed extended.

"The mother whale tries to rescue her baby that's been harpooned," Richard said, insisting on blood and gore. "But if it's dead she goes off. Whalers know about this and they wound the baby just a little bit so they can catch the mother too."

This talk of mothers and babies and wounding saddened me and I interrupted to ask Richard to tell us how much the average gray whale weighs and how deep they can dive.

He acknowledged me with a polite nod, held up one finger, and went on with his story. "And the other females help too," he said. "They're called 'aunties' and they help raise the calves."

I got up and went into the kitchen for another beer. So I am an auntie. I help to raise Ricky's calf. Richard was still talking when I came back.

"The mothers rescue the babies, the aunties rescue the babies *and* the mothers *and* each other, but if the male is harpooned nobody rescues him. Everybody just swims off."

We looked at each other, puzzled. We didn't know quite what to make of it. Then: "Easy come, easy go," said one of the grandmothers.

Chet strummed his guitar, tuned it a little, and sang most of the words to *Big Blue*. He wasn't Gordon Lightfoot but he brought that wonderful old beaten-up whale right into the living room. I saw the scars from all the near-misses and I heard the factory ships come around, aiming their explosive weapons into the harvest of soap and cosmetics and fertilizer. He blew, a slender column of vapor that reached thirty feet into the air. He saw the ships too; the blowhole disappeared and the dorsal fin broke the water, then he unfurled his flukes and *dived*, a dive too deep and too wide and too profound for anyone to follow.

Chet finished open-handed on the strings and we were quiet. Then I said I'd get the pie and ice cream, and the grandmothers came into the kitchen to help. A little while later there was talk of early rising and everyone got ready to leave.

Carol reminded Richard about brushing his teeth and not going in the water unless his dad was with him. Her eyes filled up with worry over harpoons she would not be there to intercept. Ricky put his hands on her shoulders and stooped down to look directly into her face. He made a silent promise to return to her unharmed this shared treasure, their child. It was sacred ground on which they stood—where an auntie could not go.

RICHARD WANTED TO SLEEP in the van. Ricky tucked him in while I finished in the kitchen. Later, we were strangely shy and awkward when we reached out to each other. It was the first time we would spend so many nights apart. There was little passion in our leave-taking but rather a mindfulness and regard. I was sad, partly from the free-floating melancholy produced by the whales, and partly because Ricky was going off carrying my lie with him.

He had turned over on his side but his breathing was still shallow.

"Ricky?"

"Ummm?"

"I didn't get rid of the boxes."

He turned toward me. "Yes, Megan, I know that."

"How did you know that?"

He laughed. "Because you gave up too easily. And because you've been doing a Phyllis Schlafly number for two weeks. I keep expecting you to meet me at the door in black stockings and a garter belt. I even thought you might take up walking three paces behind me. As a man's woman ought."

"Don't joke, Ricky. I need the boxes." He rolled over and turned on his light. "Why?" I asked him. "Why do they bother you so much?"

There was a frown on his face and he let out a deep, long breath. "Because," he said slowly, "because I'm afraid of them."

"Afraid?"

"It's not just the boxes, it's what they represent, it's your obsession with what's in them. I mean it, Megan, you're *obsessed*. And it scares hell out of me."

"I'm just distracted, that's all. I'm working very hard."

"You've always worked very hard. It didn't make you weird."

"What are you afraid of? I mean, what do you think will happen?"

I watched him wrestle with what looked like a terrible admission of weakness or failure. Then he said, very quietly,

"I'm afraid I'll come home some evening and you won't be here anymore. There'll be this new box . . ."

"Aw, Ricky . . ."

He ran his hand through his hair. "Look, Megan, I thought you were writing your aunt's life story. You know, for the family?"

"You mean that would be okay? Like doing needlepoint or raising African violets?"

"Now wait, that's not fair! I'd be just as concerned if you were obsessed with violets. You said you were writing down your Aunt Vida before you forgot her. That's what you said."

"That's true."

"Well then . . . God! I feel like a damn fool saying this, but why do you have to have all these people around? I feel like I've let you down, that I haven't loved you enough, that I can't give you what you need. You remember how we used to talk all the time? Well, days go by and no real words pass between us. You save your real words, Megan. You put them in those boxes. It's almost as if you had a lover."

I didn't mean to say it; it just popped out. "Maybe if I had a child I wouldn't need the boxes."

Ricky sighed and stared at the ceiling for a while. "Look," he said finally, "I know it's against our rules for me to ask you, but we've already broken the rules anyway. Do you think you could finish this . . . ah . . . project while I'm gone? Then when I get back maybe we can talk about a baby."

"Yes," I said quickly, my heart pounding so hard I could see it move the sheet up and down. "I can do that."

He smiled, kissed me, and turned off his light. It was several minutes before I realized I'd been outmaneuvered. The counselor had received a definite *yes* in exchange for a qualified *maybe*.

I turned on my light. "Ricky?"

He yawned. "Yes, Megan?"

I had nothing more to say—not really—but it seemed unfair that he should win both the argument and a good night's sleep. "Ricky. Why do we call you Ricky and your son Richard? Isn't that backwards?"

"They call me Richard at the office, and the gym, and the hardware store."

"But not your family."

He yawned again and pulled on his ear. "My mother has always called me Ricky, and my wives and girlfriends just picked up on it." He laughed. "I think they hoped to keep me small and manageable."

I flounced around in the bed. There was always a gang of females ahead of you, setting the standards, stringing the lousy cranberries for the tree. I sniffed. "Well, I think that in the future I will call you Richard."

"That could present a problem. Richard the Third, please pass the salt. Richard the Third, do not pass Richard the Second any more salt. He had high blood pressure at his last checkup."

That did it. "Now wait a minute! *I* don't tell you how to take care of yourself. As you have pointed out, it's your body and you have the legal and moral right to do whatever you want with it." Ah hah! Gotcha!

He sighed. "Yes, I know. Please excuse the ill-chosen example."

"All the same, I'm going to call you by your grownup name." It sounded like one of my nose-in-the-air pronouncements that set ears—even mine—on edge.

But Ricky only laughed sleepily. "That's a fine idea, Megan. But be forewarned, there will be times when I won't be grownup enough to answer."

He took my hand and squeezed it, and in a very few minutes I heard him dreaming of the Black Warrior Lagoon in Baja. I turned off my light and stared into the darkness for a long time. Ricky was right about real words. When had I last told him that I loved him? I sighed, turned on the itty bitty book light, clipped it to the first book on the stack, which turned out to be a Colette, not exactly comforting under the circumstances. I turned off the light and stared into the darkness some more. Off and on there was a faint droning, like bees, that came from the closet. I was awake much of the night.

RICHARD HAMMERED on our door at twenty of five. The plan was to have a ranch breakfast before they set off into the wilderness of the San Diego Freeway. I had offered to fill all requests, so while they showered and gathered their personal gear into a pile by the door, I stumbled around in the kitchen rustling up the grub: Angel's Camp sourdough pancakes, tenderfoot pan-fried steak with scrambled eggs and prairie home fries, and a side of homesteader biscuits with sausage gravy.

After this obscene repast over which I felt enormous guilt for clogging the arteries of my loved one, I walked with them down to the underground garage. It was still dark and we were the only souls stirring. Ricky was making up new lyrics to "On the Road to Mandalay."

"We'll hit dawwwwwnnnn roundabout Long Beach," he sang to Richard, making Long Beach sound like the Out Back.

"And stop for lunch (lunch?!!) at Oceanside," Richard sang back. A mere two-hour drive during which there would be man-eating tigers and killer typhoons.

I stood there waiting to wish them godspeed, but they'd been gone for hours. They climbed into the van, then quickly jumped out again and rushed to the widow's walk. Ricky gave me a big smack and a friendly pat on the rear, then stepped back. Richard came forward, grinned, and hugged me. We are almost of a size; he is large for eleven and I am small for going on thirty-two. He thanked me for the primo breakfast and said he was very glad I was a part of his family.

"I'm glad too, Richard. So very glad." He has never had any reason to suspect that I harbor a grudge against him in the names of my unborn children.

One of the reasons, I think, that this boy enjoys such

robust mental health in these bewildering times is that the adults around him treat him like a child. We are careful not to burden him with our current notions about emotional growth. I can say with some pride that we are seldom guilty of asking him to "share his feelings," and I, for one, even at the expense of syntax, have fiercely avoided, in his presence, the use of the words "meaningful" and "relationship."

There was one more quick exchange about whether some particular piece of gear was on board, then they clambered in, waved, made faces, crossed their eyes, and drove off, wheels screaming around the corner, to capture that dawn that would come up like thunder across the bay.

AS FOR ME, Megan, I hurried back upstairs, cast a baleful eye on the dishes in the sink, and headed straight for the bedroom where I threw open the closet, pushed back the caftans, and gathered up the boxes. I carried them to the living room, arranged them in a circle, and opened the lids. Turning slowly in the center, I said:

"Now then, ladies. I have something I need to discuss with you . . ."

whip, her hands punched in on her hips. "I might
happy to see you two weeks ago," she says. "I have
tuff to do, you know. We all do. We can't hang out
cking boxes while you wobble around over some

y is not *some* man," I fling back at her. "He's the
love with."

puts a restraining hand on Becky's shoulder. "You
therine's girl," she says. "You're her very image."
s at Emily. "And you have your grandmother's
er." She turns to me and smiles a halfhearted for-
People get out of sorts when they're shut up too long.
times when my family wouldn't speak to me for
ies are very demanding in that way. Now. What is
egan? What did you want to discuss with us?"
a deep breath and plunge down the mountain of
s. "I'm trying to make the most important decision
I'm trying to decide whether to have a baby." The
s in the air—small and sweet and helpless. Their
oth out and Vida nods me on. "Ricky doesn't want
children," I explain. "He doesn't even want to be
ain. But I think he would change his mind if . . ."
hat, Mary Megan?"
could make him see how important it is to me." I
aware of the lack of conviction in my voice. I sigh.
portant to me. If it's what I really want and not just
gical cliff my body wants to push me over."
l don't see what you want from us?"
nt your advice. I can't decide if it's worth it. Before
uble started, Ricky and I were happy together. We
relationship in which we were absolutely equal. We
res and expenses and concerns; we were respectful
er's individuality . . ."
s!" says Becky. "Where were you when I was look-
vell roommate?"

The Coven

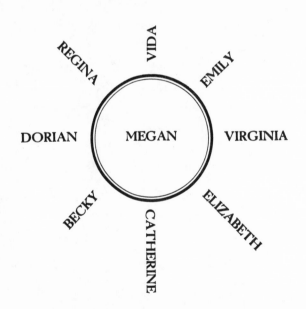

arc like a
have been
important
in these f
man."

"Ric
man I'm i

Vida
must be (
She glan
sweet tem
giveness.
I rememb
days. Fan
it, Mary

I ta
my troub
of my lif
word ha
frowns s
any mor
married

"If
"If
am acut
"If it *is* i
some bid

"I
"I
all this
had a ra
shared
of each

"J
ing for

I AM UNPREPARED FOR
eight angry women. The
corner of the room, hur
start toward them but V
eyeshade and great flowii
a traffic cop. Then, look
huddle and a circling Gr
head popping up from ti
message straight between

It is unfair of them t
But Vida just shows me
into the huddle.

"I don't understand,
see me." There is no reacti
is the loneliest place on ear
the worst kind of reproacl
own bones.

I raise my voice a not
one who has created this
thought you'd be glad to s
be happy to get out."

Becky turns toward m

Vida shushes Becky and smiles at me. "I think we get the idea."

"I mean it, Aunt Vida! A baby changes all that, even a baby there's no disagreement about. I know that! I've seen it happen with my friends, the changes. I don't know if I want to give up what we have—if we still have it. Oh, Aunt Vida, I think we may be falling out of love—if love is what we're in. And it's all my fault because of the baby. And the boxes."

"What do the boxes have to do with it?" asks Becky.

"Ricky resents the time I spend with you—all of you. He says it's an obsession."

Vida shakes her head, puzzled. "I'm sorry, Mary Megan, but I don't see how we can advise you when you have no clear idea of what you want advice about?"

"I just want you to tell me what you *think*. I believe I can benefit from your collective consciousness."

Elizabeth tugs at her sister's robe and hisses in her ear. "What's that, Vida? What is a collective consciousness? Do you know? Have you ever heard of such a thing?"

"Your collective experience," I say quickly. "Your total years of living, of learning about life and love. I thought between the eight of you, you'd know all the answers." I pause and look down at my feet. "And if all else fails I thought maybe Catherine could—well, you know—teach me to make the knots in a leather cord."

They pull amused faces at each other, then Vida bows from the waist and indicates the center of the room with her outstretched hand. "Well," she says, "I suppose we may as well sit awhile, and dole out some of our great wisdom."

They settle themselves on the couches that surround our cut-down oak coffee table on three sides, leaving Ricky's recliner at the open end for Vida. She inspects it and seems to find it to her liking, as so she should, massive and thronelike as it is. Elizabeth sits at the end of the couch on Vida's left, her knees squeezed together, feet flat on the floor, hands pinched in a bundle in her lap. Regina takes the place next to her, then Dorian and Virginia on the couch opposite Vida. Emily and Catherine take the other one, with Becky cross-legged on the floor, leaning up against her mother's knees.

Early morning light, grey and sunless, is beginning to show itself through the bank of French windows that line the east wall. I switch off one of the lamps and am wondering where I should sit when Vida asks about coffee, and maybe some muffins or doughnuts. Not to go to any trouble, whatever I have handy will be fine.

"You want to eat?"

They all nod hungrily. Becky laughs and says she's been having withdrawal symptoms over prime rib and baby carrots. Dorian speaks longingly of Paul's Mexicali Delight casserole, and Virginia ticks off the items from the menu at the Oil Rig restaurant in Tulsa.

"Of course we want to eat," says Regina. "And then could we get on with this. I have to get back to Surinam, Megan. I really must get back to work."

Feeling put upon and ill used, I grind beans and make coffee, throw together a tray of leftovers from the ranch breakfast, and heat some Sara Lee croissants from the freezer. Their voices float out to the kitchen, a muddled sound not unlike that of my mother's lady-luncheons in Dallas. This is not going the way I thought it would. One on one, as the saying goes, we are friends, equals working together, but in a group I become their servant.

When I come from the kitchen with the coffeepot and the mugs, Dorian and Regina are hard at it. It all sounds very familiar and I figure I haven't missed anything. My mother and Aunt Effie make a point of getting together at least once a year just for the purpose of reciting such a litany. They don't like to get out of practice.

"You left me with the full responsibility for Father's care," Dorian is saying. Regina tells her in a matter-of-fact tone of voice that she simply hadn't had the time to do anything about it. It is beyond Dorian's comprehension, so she says, that a child does not have time for a parent who had sacrificed so much. Regina questions the use of the word "sacrifice" in that particular situation. Dorian goes on to compare human behavior with that of animals. She speaks of compassion and generosity of spirit in the former until Regina looks as if she might throw up.

"Dorian," she says, "I was in the middle of a study I could not have left for *any* reason." She looks around the circle. "I couldn't even get sick—couldn't die!" She turns back to Dorian. "My work comes before everything. I explained that. I stated my position very clearly."

I get the trays from the breakfast bar and set them in the center of the table. "I do remember you said that, Regina," I interrupt. "You said that work was the only single-hearted companion." I bow my head under the weight of that awesome thought. "I wish I could be sure that my work would be enough for me . . ."

"And how come your work is more important than anybody else's?" Dorian hisses at Regina, completely ignoring The Help. (Get those doughnuts, tote that bale.) "I had a job," she goes on. "*And* a husband. *And* children."

"Well, of course you did," Regina says agreeably. "And you took the time to do what you felt you had to do."

"What choice did you give me?" Dorian puts an imaginary receiver to her ear. "Hello? Hello there? Los Angeles calling Deep Dark Jungle. We have a family crisis here—could you please come home?"

"I told you why I could not come," Regina says. "That was my choice to make and my guilt to live with as a result of it." She smiles wryly. "And as a side benefit, I get to watch you do Saint Dorian, the Martyr."

I set two cups of coffee down in front of them. "Ladies," I say firmly. "*I* am the one with the problem. Me—Megan Austin. Remember? I didn't mean for this to turn into a cat fight over past history."

The sisters fix me with a blood-thick glare and turn back to each other.

"I be*lieve*," Dorian announces, like someone who has just stumbled onto a great truth in the tall grass, "that you are hiding down there in that jungle, hiding behind your de-grees and your projects and your stud-eees. Hiding from people, hiding from life."

Regina narrows her eyes. "Methinks I hear the sound of dear Claudia in your voice. Methinks the two of you have gotten together for your annual sisterly lunch. Right? Was it Roasted Regina? The usual fare?"

Dorian's blink is barely perceptible. "You just think you can't get sick," she goes on, admitting nothing. "You'll get sick. Sure, and old and helpless just like Father. And who'll take care of *you*? Your precious monkeys?"

I, for one, hope Regina gives her a good one with the flat of her hand. She doesn't. She sighs with a sad patience. I can hear her thinking of that platform in the pavilion.

Regina doesn't need my help but I feel a need to give it. I put my hand on Dorian's shoulder. "Please tell me," I say to her. "I'd really like to know. Did you find it? The place you were looking for? Does a stream rush to meet you?"

She smiles, and without the armor of frowns and pouts is stunningly, glowingly beautiful. "Oh yes!" she says happily, "and the wind says my name as it passes."

I feel my breath come quickly. "If you had it all to do again," I say, "would you marry Stephen? Would you have children? Or would you—twenty years ago—go off to search for that stream?"

Her expression is at first perplexed, then faintly annoyed —that look people get when they're asked to explain the Meaning of Life or How to Clap One Hand. "Why I can't possibly answer that, Megan. I *don't* have it all to do again! And I don't have to defend what I've done." I try to frame a reply that will let her know she has mistaken curiosity for criticism, but Elizabeth, frowning and preoccupied, gets up from her place

near Vida and crosses over to sit beside Dorian. "I know exactly how you feel," she says. "Vida left too, left me with the
responsibility of the family. It's the duty of the oldest daughter
if the mother passes on—it's unwritten law—but Vida was always one to do as she pleased." She pats Dorian's hand and
they smile fondly on each other, two wronged women in the
same righteous boat.

I opened up these boxes expecting, hoping, to find wisdom, but here are the Eternal Sisters, spading up old ground,
uncovering hatchets just beneath the topsoil.

"Is that it then?" I say, wearying of my own quest. "Are
you saying that doing your duty and honoring your responsibilities are the most important things? Did that make you
happy, Elizabeth?"

Happy? Happy? Happyhappyhappy . . . It echoes through
the room and bounces off the walls.

It is Vida who speaks: "For heaven's sake, Mary Megan!
I thought you were asking about marriage and having babies.
Happiness is quite another matter. Why, we talked about what
makes people happy years ago in Tucson. Sometimes I think
you girls don't pay close attention. It was the Poetry Summer,
remember?" I shake my head that I don't remember. "Well,"
she says, "come to think of it, maybe you were too young for
Mister Rilke. He said so himself, that the young were begin-
ners, that they bungled things and had not yet understanding.
That last part's the Bible but it goes nicely, don't you think?"
She rubs her chin and speaks thoughtfully. "I guess I tried to
stretch your mind too far that summer, but I was doing my
best to lure you away from Robert and Elizabeth Browning."
She laughs and addresses the others, pointing a finger at me.
"This child," she says, "recited 'How do I love thee' that sum-
mer until I thought I'd come down with the diabetes."

It pleases me to finally be the center of attention, even as
the object of a gentle jibe. Vida could always do that: talk
about some dumb thing you had done with such affection as to
make it seem special.

"Love and Work," she says firmly. "Mister Rilke—" She pauses. "Does anyone recall his first name?"

"Ranier," Regina says immediately. "Ranier Maria."

"It's not fair for Regina to answer," says Dorian. "She has a doctorate."

"My doctorate is in biology, you twit! *You're* the librarian."

Vida leans forward, her eyes full of warning. "Regina? Dorian? You girls are just about to reach the end of my tether." The sisters eye each other with a just-wait-'til-I-get-you-outside look, then settle back obediently and fold their hands in their laps. "Now, let's see, where was I? Mister Rilke, Ranier Maria —excellent, Regina, thank you. Now this is what he said about happiness . . ."

It is on my mind to say that I'm not interested in abstractions, that I want to get back to the baby problem, but Vida is adjusting her eyeshade. It was that piece of business that told you what was coming was important and would show up on a quiz.

"He said nothing can make you happier than work, and that love, because it is the highest happiness, couldn't be anything but work." She sits back and waits for the words to sink in. "Now, Class, what kind of reasoning would you say is demonstrated in that statement?" Her students snap to attention; Regina's bright eyes stalk the question. Vida raises a restraining finger. "I am certain that you *all* know the answer, so I will call upon one of you, then we can discuss it like good Greeks. Virginia?"

"Oh, Miss Vida," Virginia laughs, "it's been a thousand years since I've thought about any of that stuff."

"Oh but you were so very good at it as a girl."

"Well, I suppose if you rearrange it a little, it could be considered deduction. All happiness requires work. Love is a form of happiness; therefore all love requires work. But I'm here to tell you, all this messing around sure as hell takes the romance out of it."

"Precisely!" cries Vida. "Romance, my dear, is play, and people have mistaken love for play when it's really very hard work. Day labor, Mister Rilke called it."

"I don't think deductive reasoning has anything to do with this," says Becky. "It assumes the premises to be true and we have no proof that they are. Deduction is like 'All men are mortal, Socrates is a man, therefore Socrates is mortal.' "

"Right," chimes in Regina. "And it can be invalid logic also. Like 'All men are mortal, sloths are mortal, therefore all men are sloths.' "

They giggle and poke at each other like fourth-graders. They are sitting here in my living room, eating my croissants, drinking my coffee, having themselves a fine old time, and they couldn't care less about my dilemma.

I begin to think about how I can herd them back into the boxes.

"I have it," says Dorian. "*If* all happiness requires work and *if* all love is a form of happiness, then all love requires work."

Becky gives a short scornful laugh. "You sound just like Megan with all those 'ifs.' "

Catherine raises her hand, and Vida nods. She clears her throat, and when she speaks her voice is shy and nervous. "It has always seemed to me—"

"I can't hear you, dear," says Vida.

"Speak up, Catherine," says Emily. "Don't mumble."

"It has always seemed to me," Catherine begins again, "that logic only proves the obvious anyway. The truth of Mister Rilke's statement is empirical, not rational. It's a generalization from a series of particular observations. It's based on wisdom and experience."

Vida claps her hands and Emily smiles approvingly on her daughter who has just walked away with the blue ribbon.

"Oh my!" cries Vida. "It's so good to be in class with you girls again!" Her pleasure shines like midday sun on the heads of her students. She does not notice that I am sulking, haven't opened my mouth since Mister Rilke appeared on the scene. "I just thought of another one," she says. "Now, who remembers this?" Her voice is breathy with excitement. "Whoever wants to have a great love in her life must collect and save for it and" —the voice drops to a throaty whisper—"and gather honey."

There are ahhhhs of appreciation if not recognition, then Emily cackles like an old crone and actually slaps her knee. Emily Cady Gladkov, of all people, slaps her knee like some hillbilly.

"*I* remember," she says. "You had it tacked up on your icebox in Cadyville." She turns to the group like someone about to share a secret. "Our Vida was a real busy bee in those days. And she did gather a *whole* lot of honey."

"Oh Em!" Vida wails. "Are you *never* going to let yourself forgive me?"

Emily looks at Vida. Vida looks at Emily. There is a heat in the room, not from anger—it doesn't sizzle or give off sparks. It is a steady heat that comes from the old charge that passes between them. I decide not to put them away after all.

"Probably not, Vida," Emily says very slowly. "Probably not. But I certainly do enjoy your company. Now, go on with the lesson."

Vida smiles, shakes her head as if she's clearing out the thoughts, then shoots straight up like someone bringing a meeting to order. "Can we reach a consensus on this matter, do you think? For Mary Megan's benefit? Everyone in favor of Love and Work?"

"Now just a damn minute here!" I say, my voice louder and harsher than I'd intended. "If I wanted to know what Mister Rilke thinks about love or work or anything else, for that matter, I'd go read Mister Rilke. And I don't *care* about rational thinking—I'm in love!" I hear what I say and have the grace to question it. "I *think* I'm in love."

Vida raises her eyebrows and with a majestic shrug slowly sinks into her chair. She gives me a royal nod that says I am to speak my piece.

It appears that I have their attention at last. "I want to know what *you* think," I say. "I don't care about philosophy or theory—we're not holding classes here. I'm thirty-one, almost thirty-two years old, and I'm worried about how many good eggs I've got left. I'm in love with a man with a bad track record who doesn't want to commit to the possibility of another failure. I want to know what to do! I have to make a choice. I *have* a work that I love—maybe that's enough." I look at Regina and she nods agreement. "But I don't know, you see? And I have love, as long as it's on Ricky's terms." Negative nods all around the circle. "I realize that some of the concerns I have, at this point in my life, are behind you. Or—" I look at Becky. "—in front of you. But surely you have some honest feelings about them." Impassive faces. Silence.

"Aunt Vida?"

"Yes, Mary Megan?"

"Why didn't you get married?"

"I chose not to."

"But you were going to marry Simon. You were happy about it."

"That's all water down the creek, Mary Megan."

"I wish you would tell me. It might help."

She looks me straight in the eye. "It won't."

"Please, Aunt Vida."

She sighs. "Simon took exception to my family. He wanted me to give them up. He said I had to choose." She is very grave. "You see? I told you it wouldn't help."

"Please go on."

"Simon had the idea that because of my devotion to my family, I would love him less. As if love were a finite quantity —if there were a quart here and a pint there and a peck here, he wouldn't get his bushel's worth." She pauses and looks first at Dorian, then at Regina. "He was a fine man, your father, but so full of fires that made ashes in his mind. He took the box and flung it against the wall. The hinge broke and the pages filled the room like white butterflies—fluttering—helpless." She looks down at the floor. "I had to get them out of there. I had to save my family." There is a long, long silence, then Vida raises her eyes. "Now then," she says briskly, "let's all put our minds to Mary Megan's problem."

Catherine's arm begins to go up and down like an exercise. "I don't know if this will help you, Megan. The only work I ever received a salary for was as a hostess in a restaurant in Culver City. It was just a job—not work as you mean." She pauses and looks sheepishly around the circle. "But I really loved being a housewife—a homemaker we called it in those days." She lifts her chin and ignores a hoot and a catcall. "I thrived on keeping a nice house and raising my children and being active in my community and a helpmate to my husband . . ."

"And look what it got you," her daughter Becky says sadly. "Dumped."

"Betrayed," her mother Emily amends, choosing a more dignified term for a circumstance they share. "And with no skills to fall back on," she laments. Emily then treats us to a short lecture on the importance of higher education. "If you had finished college," she concludes, "you wouldn't have ended up in that restaurant."

"I didn't have to work in the restaurant," Catherine says quietly. "I could have done something else. I had offers. I *wanted* to work in the restaurant."

"But why?" Becky asks impatiently. "God! Such a lousy, rotten job!"

Catherine moves restlessly, crosses then uncrosses her legs. Emily's head is inclined toward her daughter, and Becky has pulled herself up on her knees to face her. Three heads inches from each other—past, present, and future. So strong is the resemblance, it is as if one woman has posed for her portrait at different stages of her life.

I think about how it must feel for Becky to look at them and see her own smooth skin giving slack and growing porous in Catherine's face, to see her bright, clear eyes faded like a worn blue washcloth behind her grandmother's spectacles, to see her thick dark hair thinning and turning, to see her own hands gnarl up and push enlarged veins to a used surface.

To see her life pass before her.

When I look in my mirror, I see Megan Austin frozen in time someplace between twenty and twenty-five, and I've been told by older women that they too have underage reflections; that by the simple act of lowering the wattage of the light and stepping back a couple of feet, they can call up that young woman from the past, bathe and oil and perfume her, carefully make up her face, dress her smartly, then confidently take her out to dinner in a kindly lit restaurant.

But if you looked that much like someone else, then surely you were bound not just by blood, which is abstract in that sense and hidden from sight, but by flesh that won't let your mirror have its magic.

I am suddenly and overwhelmingly grateful that—even though she is beautiful—I do not take after my mother, grateful that my features came to me in such a mix it is not possible to single out an aging family donor.

Becky is pulling on her mother's sleeve, demanding an answer to her question. Catherine shakes like a leaf about to fall, and her eyes fill up with tears. She is instantly taken into a familial embrace, Emily's arm around her shoulders, Becky's circling her waist. The others round their bodies toward her. They don't bend; they *round*; ready to catch her.

She takes a deep breath, then another. "I worked in the restaurant," she says slowly, "to punish your father. A lot of our old friends came there, and people from his office. It humiliated him to have them think I had to do that. Especially after he bought the Porsche."

I stare at her, openmouthed. "Why, I didn't know that," I say.

"You mean you weren't broke?" Becky asks. "You mean Daddy helped you out?"

"He sent money. I sent it back."

"Why?"

"Because money was the only thing he knew how to give."

"I don't understand this at *all*," I say. "He came back to you. *You* sent him away. *You* returned that woman's footsteps. Why would you want to punish *him*?"

They all turn to look at me, then at each other, shaking their heads as if to say they are dealing with an idiot child. Then they round themselves back to Catherine, waiting, a gentle jury.

She tilts her head to one side, and the tears that stood in her eyes slide down her cheeks and fall on her daughter's arm. She sighs and looks at me. "I could show you how to tie those knots in the leather cord, Megan. It just takes practice. You can cause someone to stay with you, there are lots of tricks for that. But there aren't any spells to make someone love you. Not really."

"Oh, Catherine!" I cry out to her. "I'm so sorry. Listen! If you could have anything at all that you wanted, what would it be?" It is not an idle question that I put to her. At this guilt-ridden moment, I am willing to devote my life to rewriting hers.

"Don't laugh," she says, addressing all of us. "Don't make fun of me again." We nod solemnly. "I'd like to live in a big white house on a street with a lot of trees. I'd like to have someone to love and care for, to make breakfast for, to take his suits to the cleaners, to find the mates to his socks. On holidays I'd like Mother to come down from Cadyville, and my brother Gregory and his family, and my son Max and his wife . . ." She pauses and looks down at Becky. ". . . and you and your husband and children."

Becky takes her mother's hand and speaks carefully. "Max isn't married, Mom, and I don't even have a boyfriend."

"Yes," Catherine says sadly. "I know."

"Is that really all you want?" asks Emily.

"I'm sorry, Mother. I know I've been a disappointment

to you. But I never wanted to be liberated. I cherished my chains, I rejoiced in my dependence. I didn't want to be a witch either—it's a terrible responsibility, all that *power*!"

"Maybe Doctor Nettlebaum could get you a house on a street with a lot of trees," Becky says thoughtfully. "Maybe I could find a boyfriend by next Thanksgiving."

Catherine sighs and shakes her head. "No," she says in a high wistful voice. "Dr. Nettlebaum doesn't have any unmatched socks."

I glance around the circle and see all the heads nodding in measured concert. The feeling in the room is a visible, tangible thing, something you could pick up and hold in your hands. And you could say—yes, this is it, this is what sympathy feels like; it's soft and relenting; it's warm to the touch.

"You grew up in such a house," Emily reminds her daughter. "You could have come home. When he left, you could have brought the children and come home to Cadyville." Catherine looks away, and Emily sighs. "No. I suppose you couldn't have done that. I suppose you thought I'd say I told you so, that I'd known right along it wouldn't work out, that I knew that man wouldn't keep. I suppose you thought I'd go on about the importance of an education so a woman could make her own way . . ."

Catherine looks at Emily, a small knowing smile on her face. Emily meets her daughter's eyes with a defensive tilt of her chin, then nods in silent admission that yes that is what she would have done. She sighs—deeply, regretfully. Catherine's rueful smile fades into a look of profound concern. She reaches for her mother's hand. Their fingers lace together like a tightly woven basket.

As I watch them I am struck with an awful sense of loss —the loss of something I have never had. I realize that never— never once in our whole lives—have my mother and I apologized for the cruel judgment we have visited on each other.

Vida gets up and walks over to the credenza where I had

plugged in the coffeepot. She pours herself a cup, adds two heaping teaspoons of sugar and a big splash of cream, then walks over to the windows. "I think we've strayed from the question," she says. "Mary Megan—as she has had to remind us—called us here to advise her on marriage and babies." She smiles at me as if to say "You see, I'm keeping order here," but I am deep in my own thoughts. I'm thinking of the audacity, the foolhardiness I exhibit, wishing to be a mother when I have not yet learned daughtering.

Emily looks up sharply, rises, and steadies herself on her cane. She joins Vida at the window and tells her that she doesn't think they have strayed from the question at all, that babies are greening creatures who grow up and learn grief, and that it is just as real a time as when they are learning to walk, or ride a bicycle, or drive a car. "They don't stop being your children when they turn twenty-one," she says. "Or thirty. Or fifty. When they are fifty years old and coming home for Christmas and it's getting dark and the road is slick and they should have been there two hours ago—they're your children all right. It never ends." She turns and speaks directly to me. "You think about that," she says. "You can change your mind about a husband, but your children are for life."

"But Emily," I object. "You've not said one word about the joy of it—the joy of creating, of nurturing, of loving. You make children sound like a never-ending source of anxiety."

Emily thinks for a moment, then gives me a smile filled with mischief. "Anxiety does not rule out joy, Megan. It's just that the objects of your joy get themselves into earthquakes and revolutions and banks that fail. A mother's children are in constant danger.

Regina gets up from the couch and joins Vida and Emily at the window. The early-morning haze has lifted and the sun's rays strike the lower panes, spreading out in rainbows on the beveled edges, lighting the three women from behind. Their bodies are outlined in a white glow, their faces in deep shadow.

Regina extends her arms, then lets them fall slowly to her sides. She is wearing a jump suit, olive-drab and much too large for her, and her long blond hair is caught up carelessly in a rubber band. Even so, she looks like a priestess, fresh from her morning sacrifice at the temple.

"And you can't expect to have it all," she says in her clear, brisk voice. "I watched them at the university, women who had deprived themselves financially and emotionally in order to earn a Master's or a doctorate. Then, having taken the castle, they'd let down the drawbridge for the first knight who came riding by. They would marry, then because they were getting on, have a baby right away—a baby they planned to leave with an excellent live-in housekeeper while they went back to the lab or the lectern. Or they'd have worked out some scheme about sharing the upbringing with the child's father, a program that floundered at the first sign of colic or diarrhea."

There are chuckles from her listeners, but Regina shakes her head and goes on in a raised voice. "The excellent live-in housekeeper didn't last, of course. She had to go home to take care of her own children because her mother was getting too old or too forgetful or too tired to do it. There'd be another housekeeper—the pay was good and no deductions—and then another, then a sitter who came during the day and watered the Scotch.

"Finally, they'd give up and go home and comfort them-selves with thoughts of the future when the child was in school until three o'clock and they could return to work part-time. But then because it was unfair to raise an only child and because there was still little risk of producing an unsound one . . ." She smiles at me. ". . . laying bad eggs, as you put it, they would set about making more. Down the road when their lives were returned to them—used cars with a hundred thousand miles driven the opposite direction—they would make an appoint-ment with the head of the department and find that the only tenure they had was as mothers."

She holds out her hand to me. "Megan," she says, her face filled with earnest concern, "I can't advise you, I would not presume to do that, but I can tell you that I have not once, not even at three o'clock in the morning, regretted my decision to devote my life to my work." She puts her hands behind her back, smiles, and bows.

It begins as a trick of the light. The sun is shining full and brilliant on the window now. The light divides itself into a spectrum as it plays on the old beveled glass. The colors fall to the floor in circles and squares and thin bright lines. The leaves on the tree outside are moved about by a sudden breeze and their shadows cause the patterns on the floor to dance. I take in the light and the shapes and the colors and deliver them to my mind's eye. My mind's eye sends them back to me in an altered form. I feel an awful chill, a warning, but I cannot look away. I am caught between a state of terror and ecstasy as I surrender myself to the vision. I see it. I *see* it. There is a stage with heavy wine-colored drapes swept to the sides of a gold-leaf proscenium. There is an apron that juts out over an immense pit, complete with full orchestra, tuning up.

The house lights blink a warning. Dorian and Elizabeth, Becky and Catherine rise, then hurry down the aisle and up the steps to join the others. I stumble backward into a seat, third row center. The conductor raises his baton. Virginia comes to the edge of the stage and speaks to him.

"Could you hold up for just a couple of minutes? I have something to say to Megan." He taps his stand, brings a finger to his lips, and steps down off his platform. Virginia shades her eyes with one hand and peers into the darkened house. She clears her throat twice before she speaks. "I would like to say something about love."

There is a roll on the tympani and a squawk from a bassoon. Laughter from the pit. Virginia pays them no mind, just stands her ground and waits, and when everyone is quiet, she repeats, "I would like to say something about love." She

clears her throat again and squints uncomfortably across the bright footlights. "I had the Poetry Summer, Megan. It was the summer after Papa died, the last summer Vida was with us, the summer I fell in love and got broken. She was quoting Mister Rilke then too, said love was something you had to serve a long apprenticeship in, that when you got it right, you didn't go around trying to give yourself away like a pudding that would spoil if it sat out overnight."

She looks down into the pit. "I apologize for taking up your time; I'm almost finished. What I wanted to say to you, Megan, is that I regret I didn't go on and practice loving some more, didn't run the risk of getting broken again. I think if I had allowed myself some more learning time I could have let Timothy go sooner—I could have spared him some of his pain."

She steps back, and the conductor's baton strikes the metal stand with impatient little clicks. He gets up on his stool and the orchestra brings its instruments into position.

"One moment," says Elizabeth, coming forward. "I have an announcement." The conductor throws up his arms, then folds them tightly across his chest.

"There are different kinds of love," says Elizabeth. Her tone is typically defensive. "I had my chance, don't think I didn't, but not everybody wants to match up socks; but since there are folks who need their socks matched, it's good there are folks who get pleasure from doing it. I just wanted to say that I'm sorry I sent those birds away. If anybody hears of an orphan sparrow, it would be all right to give out my name." She comes to the footlights, bends over, and looks down into the pit. "I am Elizabeth Austin. I live at 1423 Elmwood Street, Apartment 201, in Tulsa, Oklahoma. Thank you for your attention."

Once again the conductor raises his baton, and this time he does not wait for interruptions. He brings it down quickly and the bell-like notes from the trumpets herald the Dance of the Sugar Plum Fairies. There appear on the stage eight little

girls in identical pink tutus. They run, heads down, to the front, search for their marks, find them, and bring one arm overhead, one to the side like a damaged wing. They seem blissfully unaware that they are out of step with the music, but they cast worried glances at each other, then switch arms, change feet. They flail, balance, and point one toe. Intensely absorbed, they bring their pink-and-white arms over their heads, their feet into position for what I recognize, from my own early years at Miss Adair's School of Dance, as a somewhat desperate relevé.

There is more running about, balancing, and toe pointing. But then, when the flutes take up the melody, bodies stretch and begin to whirl in unison with the promise of grace to come.

There are eight perfectly executed tour jetés as they leap over the awkward years. When they turn to face me in an elegant arabesque, they have grown breasts and waists and cheekbones. They glide into ever-widening circles, their eyes hooded, mysterious, their chins lifted to show long white throats.

Swelling strings—trumpets—thunderclaps. And they are joined by eight young men. In just three or four measures, they have paired off; halves of lost apples harvested from heaven at the beginning of time.

A curious thing happens: these able-bodied young women, who just moments before, and with only the music to follow, had commanded the stage, had supported themselves on their own bones, their own muscles, now are held up and led about by young men who do few twirls of their own but who are there principally as catchers.

The music descends the scale and loses its innocence. I think of my love at the Black Warrior Lagoon, of our solvency, our sanity, of our sensible life so bereft of passion, and I am filled with a yearning to be lifted, carried, transported to a place where the dance never ends. But just then the violins

announce a poignant parting. The young men pull away as if summoned to some inescapable destiny—a board meeting—a baseball game—a mistress—a war. There is an anguished extension of arms, one last interlocking of fingertips before the young men back into the wings, and the young women flutter like silver moths to the floor.

To somber chords they rise up, one by one. On flat feet they walk like a line of ducks across the stage, children and dogs trailing behind.

The burgundy drapes come together with a great swoosh. The house lights come up. I start to cry. "Is that the end?" I say in a stricken voice. "Oh please don't let that be the end!"

The conductor frowns at me over his shoulder. "Of course that's not the end, young woman. That's the first act."

WHEN THE CURTAINS part after intermission, the dancers are all wearing their everyday selves. They have gone into their football huddle again; the conductor drums his fingers on the music stand. Finally, Vida comes to the front and beckons to him.

"We've decided to do the last movement," she says.

He raises his eyebrows. "The waltz, madame?"

"Yes, that's it. Of the Flowers."

He blinks rapidly, surveys the bizarre bouquet on the stage, his eyes lingering first on Elizabeth in her tea-rose print housedress, her heavy cotton stockings, her ankles swelling out of her sturdy black shoes, then on Emily who leans heavily on her cane.

"Just the slow sections, madame?"

"Oh no," Vida answers cheerfully. "We'll do the whole nine yards. This is the best part!"

The conductor lifts his eyes to the heavens, and it is clear to me his agent will catch hell when this gig is over. He raises his arms, brings one finger to his lips for *piano*, then gently pulls the opening notes out of the oboes. The women watch Vida intently, then follow her into a deep bow. Terpsichore takes possession of their feet, lifts them, and holds them motionless through the full thirty-six seconds (I count them) of the harp solo. They come down off their toes; their movements are slow at first, tentative and studied. They watch each other for cues, frown at their own and each other's missteps. But then they find the music and they glide with it; they whirl and take a small leap—trying it out—then a bigger one, and a bigger one still. Higher and higher they soar. *They soar!* They are magical winged creatures taking flight.

But the waltz is long; the body tires and with it, its reluctant companion, the spirit—yoked as they are like oxen together. The dancers falter, stumble, and fall. They weep tears of frustration and curse their bones. The orchestra races mercilessly toward the closing notes. The women groan and gasp and help each other up. They are on their feet when the music ends.

Bravos sing out from the pit, amid thunderous applause from the audience, but Vida, laughing and trying to catch hold of her breath, signals that they will not be doing any encores.

The musicians pack up, the conductor bows low to Vida, thanks us for the fine time, and leaves his card. Vida, still breathing heavily, comes forward and sits on the edge of the stage. The others wave to me and disappear into the wings.

There is an eerie kind of quiet, that hush found only in empty theaters after a last performance. I walk slowly down to the front.

"We'll be leaving now," Vida says after an awkward silence.

"I wish you didn't have to go." My voice is small and forlorn.

She reaches down and touches my cheek. "You remember what Mister Thoreau says: that he has several lives to live and no more time for that one in Walden. Well, we have no more time for this one in Los Angeles."

I stare at her and repeat to myself what she has just said. I see the sun glimmer on both surfaces of the words and I feel the sweet edge of truth divide me through the heart and marrow.

"What is it, Mary Megan?"

"Regina's mistaken," I say, breathing fast with the exhilaration that floods through me. "I *can* have it all. Not all at the same time, but I can have it all. *I have several lives to live . . .*"

She nods thoughtfully, and I see in her eyes that indulgent look old people give to brash young visionaries. I wish you all your dreams, it says. I wish you the courage to live without them. She touches my face again and starts to get up.

I know what it will feel like when they have gone; as barren and empty and deserted as west Texas. "Can you tell me where you're going?"

She motions with her head toward the wings. "First we'll look around for a big old white house for Catherine. You'd like that, wouldn't you?" I tell her that I would like that, that at least it's a start, that indeed it would be a big load off my mind. She goes on, warming to this project. "Then we'll all go up north, spend a few days in Cadyville, then head on up to Mount Shasta and camp out for a while on Dorian's stream —she's keen on Power Circles and Medicine Wheels and Jungian psychology. It'll be good for Elizabeth, she's led such a sheltered life. After that, Regina has kindly invited us down to spend some time in her jungle. She's going to let us do some observations on her sloths. It's just a little vacation before we go back to work."

"Back to work?"

"Up to Berkeley to help out Becky; that poor child is trying to save this world single-handed." She takes a quick look around, then leans over and whispers, "Emily's going to teach her how to write fool presidents out of office."

We grin at each other like conspirators—which we are—then she pulls herself up and dusts off the back of her robe. She smiles—that most singular blessing—blows me a two-handed kiss, and starts to back away.

"I'll miss you," I say, thinking what poor, prosaic words these are for what I feel.

"I'll be around," she says.

"But it won't be the same."

"I know that. I'll miss you too."

I manage a small laugh. "I don't know what I'll do with all these empty boxes."

She's backing slowly across the stage. "Fill them up," she says.

"With what?"

"Whatever you mean to keep . . ." She's a shadow now, her words so distant I can barely hear them. ". . . Whatever you mean to let go . . ."

"Aunt Vida?" There is no answer. "Vida?"

I cover my face with my hands and when I look up the stage is gone, gone with the music and the dancers. I am sitting alone on the floor of my living room in Westwood Village. There is the sound of my breathing, of a car horn from the street, of a vacuum cleaner next door.

I sit motionless for a very long time. Listening for echos. Then I hear it, a faint, restive rustle from one of the boxes. I remember I have given my word to Ricky, and I resolutely stack up the boxes and head for the closet. But then I feel that compelling excitement that comes of someone trying to break into your mind. The drone from the vacuum cleaner stops abruptly. There is a quiet such as I have never known. Again, the rustle—louder now.

"Mother?" I whisper. "Mother, is it you?"

I WISH TO ACKNOWLEDGE the unique contribution of my own coven of women who spent the long weekend of a full moon at my house in Cambria, playing the parts of the main characters who live in this book: Kristen Barnhart, Judith Greber, Nina Sandrich, Bonnie Snyder, Elizabeth Spurr, Stephanie Spurr, Ceille Tewksbury and Kay Walker. And Joanne Wehmueller who was with us in spirit. From their lively discussions in these assumed roles came much of the material for the book's last chapter. I am fortunate to have such splendid witches as friends and colleagues. I wish also to thank my agent, Jean Naggar, and my editor at Atheneum, Patricia Lande. For critical readings and various kinds of support, I am indebted to the Cambria Writers' Workshop, to Linda Countryman and Dale Schafer at the Los Angeles Zoo, and, once again, to Ger Brody.

Jean Brody grew up in Oklahoma, was educated at the University of Tulsa and the University of California at Los Angeles, and now divides her time between Los Angeles and Cambria, a small village on the California coast. She lectures on mammals at the Los Angeles Zoo, conducts writers' workshops at Cuesta College, and works as an editor, adapting the classics for audio cassette. *A Coven of Women* is her second novel.